Ever After High™

A Semi-Charming

Kind of Life

Ever After High™

EVER AFTER
Royals!

EVER AFTER
Rebels

A Semi-Charming

Kind of Life

A SCHOOL STORY

Suzanne Selfors

LB

LITTLE, BROWN AND COMPANY

NEW YORK   BOSTON

For Isabelle

Copyright © 2015 Mattel, Inc.

Little, Brown and Company

Hachette Book Group
1290 Avenue of the Americas, New York, NY 10104
Visit us at lb-kids.com

Little, Brown and Company is a division of Hachette Book Group, Inc.
The Little, Brown name and logo are trademarks of Hachette Book Group, Inc.

The publisher is not responsible for websites (or their content)
that are not owned by the publisher.

First Edition: July 2015

Library of Congress Cataloging-in-Publication Data

Selfors, Suzanne.
  Semi-charming kind of life / by Suzanne Selfors. — First edition.
    pages cm. — (Ever After High ; 3)
  Summary: "At Ever After High, a boarding school for the sons and
daughters of fairytale characters, Darling Charming is expected to excel
in Damsel-In-Distressing class, but she yearns for adventure and envies her
brothers, Daring and Dexter, who are learning to joust in Hero Training
class"— Provided by publisher.
  ISBN 978-0-316-40136-4 (hardback) — ISBN 978-0-316-40138-8 (ebook) —
ISBN 978-0-316-40135-7 (library edition ebook) [1. Fairy tales—Fiction.
2. Characters in literature—Fiction. 3. Princesses—Fiction. 4. Sex role—
Fiction. 5. Boarding schools—Fiction. 6. Schools—Fiction.] I. Title.
  PZ7.S456922Se 2015
  [Fic]—dc23   2014047778

10 9 8 7 6 5 4 3 2 1

RRD-C

Printed in the United States of America

Contents

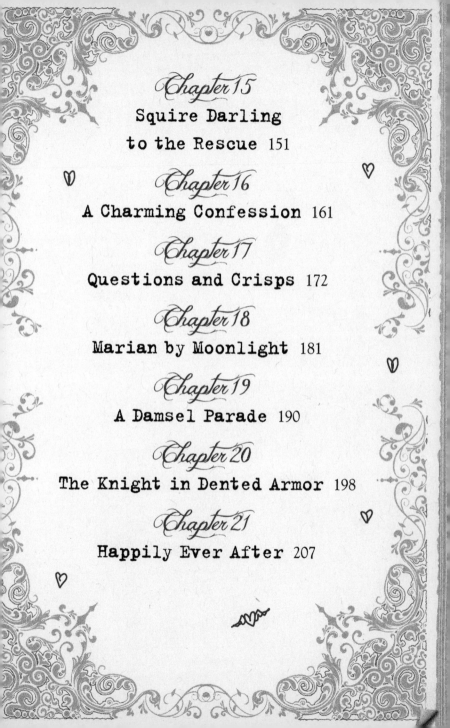

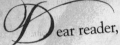

_D_ear reader,

Look for this throughout this book.

When you see it, you'll know it's a point in the story where you can rewrite someone's destiny with the companion hextbook: _Hero Training: A Destiny Do-Over Diary!_ Inside that diary are lots of activities inspired by the events of this story. Grab a copy so you can flip the script!

XO
The Narrator

Chapter 1

Beyond Boring

Darling Charming had spent her entire life *waiting*.

Perhaps that is a bit of an exaggeration, because, of course, she'd engaged in other activities, such as sleeping, eating, reading, and scrapbooking. But waiting was her least favorite thing to do, and she'd done a lot of it.

"One hour," she said. "Just one hour." She sighed. "But it feels like forever after."

"I know it's hard and it feels like a total waste of time," her roommate, Rosabella Beauty, told her. "But at least you aren't mistreated, like ogres and goblins."

Darling agreed, 100 percent. But that didn't make it any less tedious. Waiting was a traditional activity for princesses, and Darling had been taught to uphold tradition. And to be dutiful. And perfect. Such was her lot in life.

At least, that's how it appeared. At that very moment, Darling and Rosabella were sitting on the plush carpet in their dormitory room at Ever After High, a special school for the sons and daughters of fairytale characters. Their room was opulently decorated, with carved vanities, gilded mirrors, and tasseled curtains. Vases of fresh flowers sat on every available inch of counter space. This upper level of the girls' dormitory was sometimes called the Royal Wing because so many of the students who lived there were princesses. Rosabella Beauty was the daughter of the famous Beauty, a girl whose love had turned the Beast back into a prince. Darling

Charming was the daughter of the renowned King Charming, whose royal storyline stretched back to the very beginning of stories. The Charming men had always been known for their heroic deeds, luxurious hair, and enchanting eyes. Darling's two brothers were expected to follow in King Charming's heroic footsteps by saving damsels, slaying dragons, and basically conquering whatever evil stepped into their paths.

Darling, however, was not a son. She was a daughter. And being a daughter was a different matter altogether. No heroic deeds were expected of her. No quests or adventures. While the activities of the Charming princes had always been celebrated by poets and storytellers, the Charming princesses had a singular destiny—to be damsels in distress waiting for rescue. This was the way things had always been.

And because *tradition* was the first, second, and third word in the Charming motto—*Tradition, Tradition, Tradition*—this was the way things remained.

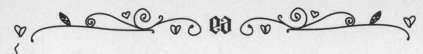

"What are you reading?" Darling asked.

"The latest issue of *Beast Weekly*," Rosabella said. As an activist who stood up for the rights of beasts everywhere, she liked to keep up with beastly matters. "Why don't you read something while you're waiting?"

"Reading is *doing* something," Darling explained as she adjusted her satin pillow. "And according to my thronework, I'm not supposed to do anything. I'm only supposed to wait." She groaned with dissatisfaction.

"That doesn't make sense," Rosabella said, tossing her magazine aside. "How can waiting be thronework?"

Darling grabbed her MirrorPad and opened her thronework app. Then she read the assignment out loud.

Class: Damsel-In-Distressing

Thronework: Waiting exercise
This week we shall practice the art of waiting, an important skill for the distressed damsel.

Instructions: Sit perfectly still for one hour. Do not fidget. Do not engage in any activities. Any and all distractions will make the waiting difficult, so clear your minds and meditate.

Points will be deducted if you fall asleep, unless you have a note from a physician stating that you suffer from a sleeping curse.

Hextra Credit: Hextra points will be given for each additional hour of successful waiting.

"Sometimes, when I stare at the wall and start counting backward, I'll stop thinking about things," Darling said with a laugh. She twiddled her polished thumbs. "I probably shouldn't be talking to you, since talking is doing something."

"I'd flip my crown if I had to take Damsel-In-Distressing," Rosabella said with a laugh. She scrambled to her feet. "I'd rather clean the bathrooms in the boys' dormitory than sit and stare at walls. I'm so glad my story doesn't require me to be a rescued damsel."

For a moment, envy washed over Darling, but she didn't say anything. She sat quietly, watching as Rosabella slipped her arms into a floral-print cardigan with a fake-fur collar. It was true that Rosabella's destiny was to be the rescuer, not the rescued. To save the beast from his horrid curse. To be the hero.

How lucky she is, Darling thought.

On the outside, the two girls seemed quite different. Raised by a progressive mother, Rosabella was outspoken, free-willed, and passionate about her beliefs. Even though she was from Royal heritage, she rarely wore a tiara. She chose comfortable, layered dresses and tall, fake-fur-lined boots rather than filigreed gowns and platform heels.

Darling, on the other hand, always dressed like a princess, in elegant clothing with nary a spot or tear. A tiara perched on her pale blond tresses, which didn't fall over her shoulders but, rather, *cascaded*, as she'd trained her hair to do. She wore just a touch of lip gloss and tried very hard to never scowl so she

6

wouldn't make a crease between her eyebrows, as she'd been taught by her mother, the queen.

But while the roommates *looked* different, on the inside, they were quite similar, though Darling was the only person who knew that truth.

"This school needs to recognize that times are changing and Damsel-In-Distressing is as old-fashioned as writing in cursive or hexpecting a fairy godmother to solve all your problems," Rosabella said as she grabbed her MirrorPad. "They might as well call the class Dozing-In-Dresses, because until you're actually a damsel in distress, waiting must get *very* boring."

Dozing-In-Dresses? Darling held back a snicker, but she secretly agreed with her roommate. "Where are you going?" she asked.

"I'm going to collect signatures. I've drawn up a petition to make it legal for beasts to eat in cafés. They should have the same rights we have, don't you think?"

"Yes," Darling said. But she wasn't sure, considering that some beasts might want to eat the cafés'

customers, along with whatever happened to be on the menu.

Rosabella opened their dorm room door, then turned and smiled at Darling. "You're welcome to join me. I could use some help."

"I can't," Darling said with a sigh. "My parents would be very disappointed if I skipped my throne-work."

"Yeah, I guess you're right. Well, see you later." And off Rosabella went.

Darling's legs twitched. She wanted to follow. She wanted to charge down the hall, dash outside, run across the footbridge, through the meadow, and beyond. But that would be unacceptable. While Rosabella's parents encouraged their daughter to speak her mind and follow her passions, Darling's parents were quite the opposite. Darling was as old-fashioned as a princess could be.

In public, at least.

Pretty Is

as Pretty Does

Because King Charming was handsome, and because Queen Charming was beautiful, it came as no surprise that when their daughter was born, everyone said, "Oh, what a pretty little thing." Darling had not only been graced with shimmering locks, chubby cheeks, and perfectly pudgy toes, but she'd also been blessed with a sweet smile and pleasant demeanor. Her parents nearly burst with pride when they introduced their lovely new baby to the people of their kingdom.

It also came as no surprise that as Darling grew, so, too, did her popularity and beauty—both inside and out. She was charming *and* a Charming. Which meant her life was charmed.

But though she learned to walk earlier than most, and though she learned to read and write earlier than most, she was praised for only one thing.

"You look very pretty."

"My oh my, what a pretty little princess."

"Prettiest princess in all the kingdoms."

"Thank you," Darling said. Then she held up a piece of parchment. "Look, I learned how to divide decimals today."

"So very, very, very pretty."

One day, when Darling was five years old, her brothers, Daring and Dexter, both covered in mud, tramped into the castle. They received a round of applause. "I've been wrestling wild boars," Daring boasted as he tugged on a leash. A massive boar grunted its displeasure as Daring led it around the room.

"Me too," Dexter said. A wild boar piglet squealed from the crook of his arm.

"Good lad," King Charming said with a slap on Daring's back. Then he patted Dexter's mud-coated head. "Good try."

But when Darling wandered out to the pigpen and wrestled a full-grown pig to the ground, she was yanked into the air by a very strong arm. Then she was set gently onto the ground. "What do you think you're doing?"

She stared into her father's narrowed eyes. "I'm wrestling," she told him. "Just like Dare and Dex."

"A princess does not roll around in the mud with pigs," he informed her.

"Why not?" she asked.

"Because that pig is three times as big as you. You could have been squished!" He shook his head. "Rolling around in the mud. Honestly, you should know better." He carried her into the castle and deposited her into the arms of her nursemaid. "Bathe the princess at once."

When her brothers limped into the castle with gashed knees, their britches torn, they received another round of applause. "I climbed to the top of Ogre Mountain and planted the Charming flag," Daring said, his rope and safety hooks slung over his shoulder.

"I made it halfway up," Dexter said with a shrug.

"That's my boy," King Charming said with a slap on Daring's back. Then he patted Dexter's shoulder. "Better luck next time, son."

But when Darling skipped out to the meadow, hiked up her skirt, and climbed the tallest tree at Charming Castle, she found herself staring down at her father's scowling face.

"What do you think you're doing?" he called up to her.

"I'm climbing, just like Dare and Dex."

"Come down this instant. A princess does not climb trees!"

"Why not?" she asked as she shimmied down the trunk.

"Because you could fall and get hurt! You should know better." He carried her into the castle and deposited her with the royal seamstress. "Mend the princess's dress at once."

Later that night, the queen visited Darling's room. She sat next to her on the canopy bed and gently took her chin in her hand. "My precious daughter," the queen said. She smelled of lilac blossoms, and her golden hair was swept into a towering beehive. "I know it seems unfair that your brothers get to tromp all over the place, doing whatever they please, while you must stay indoors and sit quietly. But that is the way it has always been and the way it must always be."

"Why?"

"Your brothers must grow big and strong and face dangers so that they can become heroes. But you must wait patiently, look pretty, and behave in a ladylike manner. A princess cannot possibly come across as charming if she is covered in mud or if her dress is torn. My mother always told me, 'Pretty is as pretty does.'"

Pretty is as pretty does? Darling thought long and hard about that statement. Then she frowned at her mother. "Everyone tells me I'm pretty and well liked, but what good is it if I'm not allowed to do *anything?*"

"That's not entirely true," Queen Charming said. "You can work on your conversation skills, develop your personal style choices, and master the art of scrapbooking. And when you go to school, you will follow a rigorous course of study that will prepare you for the big day."

"Big day?" Darling asked, sitting up super straight. She pushed aside her stuffed fairies. This was the most exciting news she'd ever heard. "There's going to be a *big day?*"

"Of course." The queen patted Darling's hand. "The day your prince arrives."

Darling didn't quite understand. "You mean I'm going to have a visitor?"

"Yes, a very important visitor from a faraway kingdom. And when he arrives, he'll rescue you."

"How come he's got to rescue me?" Darling asked. "Is something bad going to happen to me?"

"Yes," she said matter-of-factly. "But that is how it has always been with Charming princesses. A dragon will abduct you, or an evil sorcerer will curse you, or you might even get locked in a tower, though that seems a bit overdone these days." The queen smiled. "But fear not, because your prince will rescue you. Then he'll proclaim his true love and marry you, and you'll live happily ever after in a castle just like this one. But until that day arrives, your father and I must do our best to keep you safe. Now, sleep well, my darling."

Darling did not sleep well. In fact, after hearing such news, she couldn't sleep one wink. So, after the castle candles had been extinguished and her parents had gone to bed, she tiptoed down the hall to her brother Dexter's room.

"Dex, I can't sleep. Mother says that something bad is going to happen to me and I'll need to be rescued."

Dexter was playing the latest version of *Troll Quest* on his MirrorPad. "Don't worry," he told her. He patted the bench and she sat next to him. "I'll come to your rescue."

"You will?" she asked. "You promise?"

"Of course I promise. I'm a prince, after all. Why can't I be the one to rescue you?"

"Thanks," Darling said. "And if you ever need help, I'll rescue you."

"It's a deal." Then, taking turns on his device, they made their way through the Screaming Swamp until they defeated the troll king. And even though she was only five years old, Darling realized that she and her brother made a great team.

Strong Is

as Strong Does

As soon as Rosabella's footsteps had faded down the hallway, Darling jumped to her feet and slid the dead bolt on the door. Go ahead—let the outside world believe she was sitting around, waiting. But forty-five minutes remained in her thronework assignment, and she wasn't going to let that precious time go to waste.

She opened her closet, reached into the very back, and pulled out a piece of clothing. It was not a gown dripping in jewels or a summer frock spun from

gossamer silk. And it had not been approved by the Charming Committee on Appropriate Apparel. This was a suit made of lightweight, breathable, sweat-resistant material that had been woven in the Elvish District. She'd saved her coins to order it off the Mirror Network, and she'd had it delivered to the school. Such an outfit would have been forbidden at Charming Castle. Athletic wear didn't fit her parents' standards for proper princess attire.

But it felt so comfortable and moved like a second layer of skin. After slipping into the silver pants and white tank top, she removed her tiara, pulled her hair into a ponytail, then proceeded with her workout routine. She began with thirty push-ups, fifty sit-ups, and ten chin-ups on the bar in her closet. Then she started her lunges. Finding the time to exercise was always tricky, since she had to do it in solitude. But it felt so good to move!

Thump.

A bouquet of field flowers had soared through the open window and landed next to Darling's feet.

Receiving a bouquet was a daily occurrence for Darling, which was why her dorm room looked and smelled like a florist's shop. "Darling Charming, are you in there?" a boy called. "Those flowers are for you!"

Not wanting to be seen in her workout clothes, she stuck her hand out the window and waved. "Thank you," she called. It was the polite thing to do, but honestly, she was sick of the attention. Because she was the only girl in the Charming family, boys were always trying to woo her in an effort to prove themselves worthy of the Charming family charm and secure their role as famous princes. It must have been tiresome. Even the cleaning fairies complained about having to haul away the bouquets when they started to wilt. The only person who seemed to appreciate the constant supply of flowers was not a person but a butterfly named Adelita. She belonged to Rosabella, and she loved to spend her days perched on the petals, drinking nectar. Darling's pet, a horse named Sir Gallopad, never stayed in their room. He spent his nights in the school's stables.

"I love you!" the boy yelled. Darling frowned. Whoever he was, he didn't actually love her. Real love was not about wanting to nab a princess just because her last name was Charming. Real love was much deeper. But she didn't blame the boy for his declaration. She loved being a Charming more than anything in the world, and she could see why every boy in the kingdom would want to be part of her royally cool family. Luckily, the giddiness wore off eventually, and when it did, the poor besotted fellow could go on with his life.

"I've never felt this way before!" he hollered, his voice cracking. "I want to be your Prince Charming! Will you marry me?"

"No, I won't marry you," she called. She'd long ago decided that honesty was best. Why give him false hope? "But thanks for asking." She closed the window. The boy had probably noticed her that morning, when she'd walked to the Castleteria for breakfast.

Darling stuck the bouquet into a vase, then returned to her routine. Squats were next, followed by jumping

jacks. The space between the two beds provided ample room for her exercises. Over the years, she'd taught herself to work out in small spaces. It would be too risky to use the athletic field or the Grimmnasium. If she was seen, someone might report back to King and Queen Charming that their precious daughter had been engaging in—*gasp!*—physical activity. "A princess should be healthy," her father had said. "But overactivity is unnecessary and can lead to cramps, heat exhaustion, and an unsightly development of muscles. Besides, a princess doesn't need to be strong. She can leave that to her rescuer."

Darling flexed her right bicep, then her left. She smiled. This princess was strong!

Just as she finished her squats, her MirrorPhone alarm rang, indicating that the thronework hour had passed. She took a swig of Rip Van Winkle Vitamin Water. Rosabella would be gone for a while. She could probably fit in another hour of "waiting."

But a noise drew her attention. She quickly changed back into her dress before stepping onto

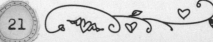

the balcony. Gentle sunlight warmed her arms and cheeks as she leaned against the stone railing. In the distant field, beyond the swan pool and the rose garden, the Hero Training class was in progress. Professor Knight sat on horseback, waving his arms as he lectured his students. Each student wore a suit of plated armor. It was clearly the first time many of them had worn such a getup, for they were teetering around and bumping into one another. Darling chuckled to herself. They looked silly, but at least they got to *do* something. Heroes were never told to sit around and wait.

But then the class took an interesting turn. A horse was led onto the field. Professor Knight, an elderly knight who'd been teaching at Ever After High since the previous century, pointed at the group of students. Darling gripped the balcony rail as two boys stepped forward. Both boys wore helmets, so she couldn't tell who they were. She squinted. The taller boy had a painted ax on his breastplate. That could only mean he was Hunter

 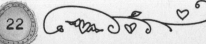

Huntsman, son of the Huntsman, who had rescued many damsels in distress, including Snow White and Red Riding Hood. A capital C was painted on the other boy's breastplate. C for *Charming*. It was one of her brothers—but was it Daring or Dexter?

Professor Knight hollered some directions. With the assistance of another student and a step stool, Hunter mounted the steed. He wobbled a bit in the saddle but managed to find his balance. Then he rode in a tight circle and dismounted. It couldn't be easy to ride with all that armor weighing him down. Darling knew that Hunter was skilled at hunting and tracking on foot, but she'd had no idea that he could ride so well.

Then it was her brother's turn. Surely, this would be an easy feat for either brother. As soon as they could walk, both Charming boys had been trained to ride horses. Daring was their kingdom's most dec-orated rider, having won blue ribbons every year at the Charming County Fair. Though Dexter had never won a championship, he was moderately good. "Don't fret," Queen Charming had always told her secondborn son whenever her firstborn son brought home another blue ribbon. "You don't have to be the best. You only have to be *second* best."

Down on the field, Darling's brother took a few steps. He wobbled as he walked, weaving left, then right. Finally he reached the horse. But instead of stepping onto the stool, he bumped right into the horse and fell over. The students began to laugh.

Darling sighed. There was no doubt about it—the brother wearing the armor was Dexter.

Dexter lay on his back like an overturned tortoise. He rolled to one side, then to the other, but was unable to get up. A couple of students grabbed his hands and pulled him to his feet. He tilted, unsteady. Was the weight of the armor throwing him off balance? Darling watched, wide-eyed, as Dexter reached out his hands and felt his way around the horse. What was the matter with him? He wasn't usually such a klutz. Had he stayed up all night gaming? Maybe he hadn't been taking his royal vitamins.

After being helped onto the stool by two students, then pushed onto the horse, Dexter was finally sitting upright in the saddle. But just as Darling was about to sigh with relief, he toppled over and landed in the grass, flat on his back again. She winced. That armor was clearly not agreeing with him. Another student stepped forward. He took off his helmet, revealing a mane of golden-blond hair. It was her brother Daring. He helped Dexter to his feet.

A knock on the door was an unwelcome distraction, since Darling was worried about Dexter. "Just a minute," she called. She undid her ponytail and wiped perspiration from her nose. She checked her reflection to make sure everything was *cascading* and shine-free. Then she opened the door to find Apple White, daughter of Snow White, patiently waiting. "Sorry that took so long. I was…powdering my nose."

"No problem," Apple said in her chirpy way. "I don't mind waiting. Waiting is our thronework assignment, after all." She looked as lovely as ever, in an apple-red dress. Her pet snow fox, Gala, was curled around her neck, fast asleep. "These are for you." She handed three envelopes to Darling. "They were delivered to my room by mistake."

Darling didn't need to look at the envelopes. While some boys bought flowers, others wrote love letters—super-corny love letters. How hextremely embarrassing! Darling tossed them into a basket that was already brimming with mail.

Apple raised her eyebrows. "As the fairest in the land, I adore getting love letters. Aren't you going to read yours?"

"Eventually," Darling said. But the truth was, she was sick of reading those letters. They all said the same thing. *You are the prettiest, yack, yack, yack. My heart beats for you alone, blah, blah, blah. I will be your Prince Charming, yadda, yadda, yadda.*

"Do you need the number for the dwarf who handles my publicity?" Apple offered. "He's great at answering fan letters, love letters, hexts, smoke signals, pigeon parcels, and such. As crowned princesses, we have a duty to our subjects, even if our subjects are a tad hexhausting sometimes."

Darling sighed. Though Apple was nice, she had a tendency to only see things the Royal way. "I know what I'm *supposed* to do," Darling said. "But seriously, why should I get stuck answering all these letters? These boys are only writing to me because I'm a Charming. There are so many other things I could be *learning* and *doing* with my time."

"I understand." Apple adjusted her tiara. "But do you know how many girls would love to have your destiny?"

"They can have it," Darling said. "If I could swap with them, I would."

Apple gasped. Then, after looking around, she stepped into the room. "Don't say things like that.

People might think you're a *Rebel*." This year at Ever After High, the word *rebel* had a lot of buzz around it. It was used to define a student who openly questioned his or her storyline—who spoke out about destiny not being written in stone, but being written by choice. It was a new philosophy that shocked many of the older generation, including Darling's parents. And it was a subject Darling wanted to avoid. So she was grateful when cheering arose from out on the field.

"What's that?" Apple asked. The snow fox opened her eyes and lifted her head.

"Hero Training class," Darling said. "They're learning how to ride in a full suit of armor."

"Oooh…that must mean they're going to joust." She clapped her hands. "I love a good joust. Remember how Daring won last year? He'll be champion again, of course."

It went without saying. Daring was always the best when it came to being a hero.

Apple White's fairytale destiny was to marry a Prince Charming. Though there were many Prince Charmings, it was naturally assumed that Daring and Apple were destined to be together, happy forever after.

Apple hurried out onto the balcony. Darling followed. Hero Training class appeared to be over. Professor Knight had departed, and the other students were leaving the field. But one student was sitting in the grass like a lump. He removed his helmet.

"Why's Dexter just sitting there?" Apple asked as she stroked her snow fox's tail.

Before Darling could respond, Apple's Mirror-Phone chimed.

"Oh dear, I'd better go. Daring and I have a lunch date at the Beanstalk Bakery. There's a new doughnut named after him. Daring's Doughy Delight. It will be delicious, of course." She blew Darling a kiss, then hurried to the door. "Charm you later," Apple said. The snow fox waved good-bye. And off they went.

Darling looked back at the field. Dexter hadn't moved. Something wasn't right. He needed her.

It would take exactly twelve minutes to walk down all the staircases and hallways of the school before reaching the garden below. She could run it in two minutes. But because she was a Charming princess with a traditional reputation to uphold, running in public, in the middle of the school day, was out of the question. Plus she didn't want to draw more attention to Dexter's plight. Most likely he was feeling sorry for himself. The last thing he needed was a bunch of students rushing to his side, asking him why he couldn't ride a horse like his brother. So she closed the dorm room door. Then she set her tiara onto her head, secured it with a few hairpins, and stepped back onto the balcony. The quickest way out of the dormitory was down. Straight down.

She peered over the railing. The boy who'd tossed the bouquet had wandered off. No one else was around. She had to be quick. She grabbed one of the vines that grew up the school's stone walls. It wasn't as thick as a beanstalk, but it was sturdy enough to hold her weight. This wasn't the first time she'd used this method of travel. In fact, over the years, she'd become quite the expert climber. But that was another one of her secrets.

King Charming was the reason Darling had begun climbing, for he was the one who'd sent her to *the tower*.

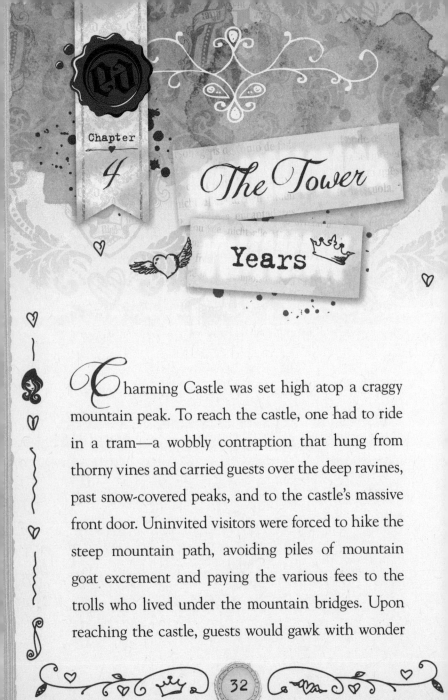

The Tower

Years

Charming Castle was set high atop a craggy mountain peak. To reach the castle, one had to ride in a tram—a wobbly contraption that hung from thorny vines and carried guests over the deep ravines, past snow-covered peaks, and to the castle's massive front door. Uninvited visitors were forced to hike the steep mountain path, avoiding piles of mountain goat excrement and paying the various fees to the trolls who lived under the mountain bridges. Upon reaching the castle, guests would gawk with wonder at the splendor of its design. Framed with massive timbers brought in by the giants, and built with glacier stones, the castle withstood storms, quakes, and the occasional onslaught of dragon fire. And poking out of the top of the castle was a tower.

The tower consisted of a narrow staircase that led to a grand turret, a decent-sized room that provided breathtaking views of the mountain range, the winding river, and the village and farmlands below. During most of Darling's life, this room had been filled with cobwebs, alarmingly large spiders, and the occasional wandering pixie. Darling never suspected that such a gloomy place would become her bedroom.

Or her prison, depending on one's point of view.

The chaos began one evening while the Charming family was sitting down to supper. As the servants scurried around the grand table, plopping dollops of whipped butter onto crusty sliced bread and ladling soup into golden terrines, a loud knocking arose at the front door.

"Sire," the butler announced with a bow. "A young lad is at the door, requesting the princess's hand in marriage."

Darling's mouth fell open. "Did you say my hand in *marriage?*" she asked the butler.

"I did indeed, my princess."

The servants froze. A moment of silence filled the dining hall. Then Daring and Dexter flung themselves from their chairs and raced out of the room, shoving and pushing each other to see who could get to the door first. The king was close behind. Darling, who was not supposed to run, because it increased the likelihood of falling and breaking a bone, lifted her skirt and speed-walked as quickly as she could, accompanied by her mother, the queen. By the time they reached the front door, it appeared that everyone in the castle had gathered—pantry maids, stable hands, even the old man who cleaned the royal chimneys. Darling squeezed between her brothers to get a better look.

A boy stood on the stone steps. He was panting like a racehorse and holding a bouquet of charm blossoms. He wore ordinary, village-mall clothing. No crown sat upon his head. When he saw her, he fell to one knee. "Will…you…?" He gasped for air. "Sorry. That trail…was very…steep." He wiped sweat off his brow. "Princess Darling, will you marry me?"

Everyone turned and gawked at Darling. She wasn't sure what to do. The king narrowed his eyes. "Do you know this boy?" he asked her. He was still holding his salad fork.

"No," she said, for she'd never seen the boy before in her life.

"I work in the village," the boy explained. "My father owns the Magic Bean Shop." He grinned at Darling in a goofy sort of way. "I saw you walk by this morning. I have long admired the Charming family, and I knew the instant I saw you that we were meant to be together."

Darling cringed. Her cheeks grew hot. It was true that she had gone for a walk in the village with her brother Dexter. But she didn't remember meeting this boy. How could he possibly want to marry her?

King Charming cleared his throat. "See here, young man." As he waved his fork around, a piece of tomato flew off and landed on the butler. "I'm sure your father is a very reputable merchant, but my daughter is a princess and thus will marry someone with a royal title. Besides, she is not yet of marrying age and—" Before he could explain further, another boy barreled up the steps, equally sweaty and equally out of breath. A heart-shaped box was tucked under his arm.

"Princess Darling, will you marry me?" he pleaded as he fell to one knee.

"Hey, I asked her first," the boy said, delivering a sharp elbow jab to his competitor.

"Yeah, but I am truly destined to marry into this family," the second boy insisted. "I am far more worthy of the Charming princess than you are!" They began throwing punches. Darling couldn't believe her eyes. What was going on? Were they fighting over her?

"That's enough!" King Charming ordered. "No one is marrying my daughter! Go back to the village." Then he spun on his heels and pointed at Darling. "And you, young lady, get back inside."

Darling felt terrible. But what had she done? She hadn't spoken a single word to either boy. How could they think she would marry them? While her brothers chased the boys away, Darling followed her mother inside. "Why were they acting so weird?" Darling asked.

Queen Charming wrapped an arm around Darling's shoulder and explained. "You are older now, and as you have grown, so, too, has your beauty and charm. Our family is well known throughout the kingdom, and there are many, many boys who will want to prove their worth by marrying a Charming princess. Especially one as lovely as you!"

"Yuck," Darling said with a roll of her eyes. "That's gross."

And thus it continued. If Darling took a ride to visit relatives, or attended a ball or feast in another village, the very next day a constant stream of suitors would appear at the castle door with flowers, chocolates, and the occasional stuffed unicorn. Bouquets lined the hallways. Love letters filled the royal mailbox. Even trolls and ogres came courting.

"Can't a king enjoy his supper in peace?" King Charming hollered one night after they'd been interrupted for the fifth time. "Sons, defend your sister from these adolescent intruders!"

From that moment on, Daring and Dexter didn't simply chase away the suitors; they made a sport of it. Dexter rigged buckets over the front door. A dousing with cold water was especially effective. Daring preferred chasing them with his sword drawn or charging on his trusty steed. Of course, no one was hurt in the process, but it was best to deal with the fame-seekers swiftly, to discourage them from setting up camp. And if they started singing corny love songs below Darling's window, the royal hounds were released.

The royal sign-maker was summoned to carve a sign from the finest mahogany for the front door.

> ## THE PRINCESS IS NOT ACCEPTING MARRIAGE PROPOSALS AT THIS TIME.

But despite these efforts, boys continued to show up on the doorstep. And when one was found stuck in the chimney, King Charming called a family meeting. "My darling," he said, "the suitor situation has gotten out of hand. Thus I have decided that you must stop venturing outside the castle."

"You want me to stay inside?" Darling asked. "But I thought you wanted everyone to see me. I thought you were proud of me because I'm so charming."

"We are proud," he said. "But circumstances have changed. Until it is time to send you to Ever After High, you must spend your days inside, out of sight from all those pimple-faced boys. Your spellementary teacher will come here to teach you. That should calm things down for a while." He wagged a finger at

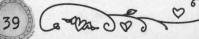

her. "And don't even think about sneaking to the village. If I have to listen to one more screechy version of 'Girl, You Rock My World' being sung outside the dining room window, it will be 'off with their heads' like the Queen of Hearts!"

So, in an attempt to keep the peace, the king had Darling's bedroom moved to the grand turret in the castle's tower. The servants cleared away the cobwebs, spiders, and a few pixie squatters, then set up a canopy bed. "This is so cliché," Darling grumbled, plopping herself onto a velvet chair. "Seriously? I'm going to be a princess stuck in a tower? How many times have we heard *that* story?"

"Sweetie," Queen Charming said as she checked her reflection in one of the many mirrors that now decorated the room. "You are not *stuck* in a tower. You are simply living here. Most of the time. And not leaving unless you have permission."

Though it felt like the worst-case scenario, it took only a few days for Darling to realize that tower living had its benefits. Firstly, she had to climb a long flight of stairs, so her legs grew strong. Secondly, because most everyone hated climbing those stairs, she had long stretches of time completely to herself. With no one paying any attention, she made weights out of stacked books. She used the rafter for pull-ups.

Why did she bother with these activities?

Because Darling had realized that in all those stories about girls stuck in towers, not a single girl had simply climbed out. Which seemed the most logical thing to do. So Darling decided to build up her strength. By moonlight, she shimmied out the window and taught herself how to climb the ivy trellis. Within a few months, she was scaling the wall as gracefully as a spider. And beneath her delicately woven gowns and lacy festive frocks, Darling became transformed. She now possessed a body as strong and sinewy as any athlete's.

Living in a tower might have been an old-fashioned story, but Darling Charming was rewriting it.

Dexter's

Dilemma

Back at Ever After High, Darling climbed down the vine and jumped onto the grass beneath her balcony. She wanted to kick off her shoes and sprint at full speed, her hair whipping behind her like a horse's mane. But she controlled this urge, instead walking briskly, her chin held high and shoulders back as she'd been taught. "Never stomp, never slink, never skedaddle," her mother often said. "A princess must *glide*."

Gliding was a royal pain, but thanks to her athletic prowess, Darling had mastered the technique

of gliding quickly, her feet barely skimming the ground, as if she were supported by fairy wings. As she made her way past the school's bookstore, a pair of boys got so distracted trying to attract her attention that they bumped into each other. Another boy tripped over is own feet when, after realizing he had just walked by the daughter of the Charming family, he tried to double back and run after her. Bike tires screeched. Something was knocked over. *I'm a walking natural disaster*, she thought.

She reached the school gardens, which were as lovely as could be, with shrubbery sculpted like dragons, unicorns, and griffins. There were sparkling fountains, velvety roses, and lazy pools of shade beneath willow branches. The blue sky was highlighted by faint streaks of fairy dust. Students sat on benches around the swan pond, chatting and checking their MirrorPhones. A few members of the cheerhexing squad flew past, their pom-poms rustling like leaves. Ashlynn Ella, daughter of Cinderella, and Hunter were stringing a banner between two stone pillars.

WELCOME TO PARENTS WEEKEND

Darling had forgotten about Parents Weekend, an annual school event. But she didn't have to worry, because her mother and father would be away, having already scheduled a cruise to Avalon. The fact that her parents couldn't attend was a huge relief. It would have been quite stressful to have King and Queen Charming following her around all weekend, checking to make sure she was being the perfect princess and that she wasn't engaging in any dangerous activities. How would she explain the calluses on her hands from the ivy vines?

"Hi, Darling!" Cedar Wood, daughter of Pinocchio, waved to her. Darling waved back, fanning her hand through the air as she'd been taught. She'd already aced the waving thronework in Damsel-In-Distressing. But there was no time to stop and chat. Dexter was still sitting in the middle of the field. He needed her.

At that very moment, a tall man caught her eye. Headmaster Grimm was strolling along the path, as

 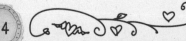

he often did, stopping to check in with students. Darling tried to dart around a glass-slipper-shaped shrub, but she wasn't fast enough.

"Ms. Charming," he called. He usually referred to the students in this manner, choosing not to call them by their royal titles. While at Ever After High, each student was equal to any other student. In theory, at least.

"Good morning, Headmaster," she said as she glided to a stop.

He was wearing far too many layers for such a nice day, but that was his style. The high-collared shirt, the waist jacket, the coat with tails, and the cravat gave him a gentlemanly air. "You are well, I presume?"

"Yes."

"Hexcellent news." He ran a hand over his gray mustache. "Your father called yesterday to check on your status. I assured him that even though we have not locked you in a tower, you are most safe here on campus. Our high-tech security system is on alert

each evening. No starstruck intruders will princess-nap you—not on my watch." He clasped his hands behind his back.

Campus security was tight, but Darling had two personal security guards of her own—her brothers. Daring could often be found chasing suitors off campus. Sometimes, Dexter would even sleep on the floor outside Darling's room.

"Learning to live with constant suitors is your lot in life, and it is best that you deal with it, instead of hiding away in a tower. We must each learn to live with the hand we've been dealt, wouldn't you agree?" Headmaster Grimm was a firm believer that one should follow one's storyline.

"Yes, I wholeheartedly agree." But that didn't mean she had to like it.

He smiled approvingly. "I look forward to seeing your mother and father during Parents Weekend."

"Oh, they won't be coming," she said. "They've booked a stateroom on Mermaid Cruises."

"That is disappointing news. Your father is our school's most generous benefactor, and I was going to hit him up for…er, I mean *request* a small contribution to Hagatha's retirement fund. The sooner she retires as lunch lady, the sooner our stomachs will recover. Well, good day, Ms. Charming."

"Good day." She waited patiently until he was out of view. Then she crossed the drawbridge and headed onto the field.

Dexter hadn't moved. He sat with shoulders slumped, staring down at his feet. His helmet lay on the ground. Since there was no velvet pillow or stool to perch upon, she plopped onto the grass next to him. "Hi," she said. "Are you okay?"

"Hi," he grumbled, not bothering to look up. He had a bad case of helmet hair, and his armor was dented. And on top of that, he sounded congested.

"What's the matter?" She didn't want him to know that she'd witnessed him falling off the horse, in case he didn't want to talk about it. But she knew, from his tight expression, that he was feeling defeated.

He ripped a buttercup from its roots. "We're learning how to joust, but I can't even get onto the horse!"

"Look on the bright side," Darling said. "You *get* to joust. Guess what I have to do for my class. I get to wait. That's right—I get graded on sitting and doing nothing."

Dexter winced. "That's the stupidest thing I've ever heard."

"Tell me about it." She laughed, because sometimes her predicament was downright funny. "Right now, I'd trade your thronework for mine in a heartbeat."

"I can't trade. We're going to have a tournament for Parents Weekend. It's tradition." He groaned. "How can I compete in a tournament? I'm terrible."

"It's just the first day. You can't be perfect on the first day."

Dexter's shoulders slumped again. And then he said exactly what she had expected he'd say. "Dare was perfect on the first day."

Even though Darling hadn't witnessed her oldest brother's first day of riding lessons, she knew he'd pulled it off without a hitch. Life was easy for Daring. Whether graced by luck or skill, he never failed when it came to being heroic. Daring's perfection was one of the reasons why Dexter and Darling had grown so close during their childhood. While she'd been raised beneath a canopy of strict rules regarding her appearance, her manners, and her daily routine, Dexter had been raised in his brother's shadow.

Daring Charming was everything his mother and father had hoped for and more. Handsome of face, strong of body, and brave of heart, he was the model of a perfect Charming prince. A skilled swordsman, an elegant equestrian, and a terrific tower climber, he possessed all the skills required of a hero. Girls swooned for him. Boys wanted to be him. But no matter how hard Dexter tried, he couldn't match his brother's accomplishments.

Daring was number one, and Dexter was, well, number two.

They were different in other ways, as well. Daring knew he was handsome, and his grooming routine was elaborate and time-consuming. Like his pet peacock, P-Hawk, he enjoyed being seen. He was confident and could march into any room and begin a conversation, even if he knew nothing about the subject.

Dexter, on the other hand, wasn't arrogant about his good looks. His tousled mop of chestnut hair gave him a more casual style than his brother, and his dreamy eyes were often hidden behind a pair of black-framed glasses. He preferred to observe and form his opinions before sharing them. He was thoughtful, intelligent, and sweet. But though he possessed all those amazing attributes, there was always the sense that he wasn't measuring up to King Charming's expectations.

"So what if Dare was perfect on the first day?" Darling said. "You've got to stop comparing yourself." How many times had she said that over the years?

"Look, I know you're trying to make me feel better, but you don't know the half of it."

"The half of what?"

"I'm having trouble because my glasses don't fit under the helmet. And you know I can't see two feet in front of me without my glasses." He frowned. "But that's not the worst part."

"What's the worst part?"

He picked up his helmet. Then he sneezed.

"Are you getting sick?"

"No." Dexter sneezed again, then he set the helmet back into the grass. "I think I'm allergic to armor!"

Chapter 6

Overly

Perfect

"You can't be allergic to armor," Darling said, though she wasn't so sure. When he was a little boy, Dexter had been allergic to cat dander, golden goose feather pillows, and pixie pollen. Fortunately, a round of royal allergy shots had cured him.

"It has to be an allergy. My nose got stuffy the second I put on the breastplate and backplate."

"It's just a coincidence," she said, trying to sound convincing. If her brother was indeed allergic to

armor, the quintessential outfit for a hero, he'd never live it down. "You're probably catching a cold."

"Maybe." He sneezed a third time. "But whether I'm sick or not, I'll still be a total failure at jousting. I'm liable to ride in the wrong direction, or worse— skewer an innocent bystander!" He took off his glasses and rubbed his eyes.

Though Darling knew her brother's face by heart, she was always surprised when he removed his glasses. When it came to piercing eyes, Dexter Charming reigned supreme. It wasn't just the rich blue color, or the lashes as thick as paintbrushes—the eyes themselves sparkled. They twinkled. They were simply to die for. But there was one slight flaw, and this was discovered on the day he learned to crawl.

"Why does he keep bumping into the walls?" the queen whispered worriedly to her husband. "Is something the matter with our baby boy?"

"That's not possible," King Charming told her. "Charmings are well built and athletic."

The royal physician was summoned, and after bandaging the boy's head, he declared, "I am very sorry to tell you this, Your Majesties, but it would appear that your son has…" He paused. "Imperfect vision."

"Imperfect?" King Charming leaped to his feet. The pitiful physician began to quake. "Did you call one of my children *imperfect?*" Right on cue, Dexter, who'd been crawling around his mother's feet, bumped his head on her throne.

"No, Your Highness of Royalness and Magnificence," the physician said. "What I meant to say was that his eyesight is…*overly* perfect."

"Of course it is," the king said proudly. He sat back on his throne. "Overly perfect eyesight. Do you hear that, my dear? Our son is more than perfect. He is overly perfect."

"Yes, that does make sense," the queen said. "But what do we do about all the lumps and bumps on his head?"

"He shall require…lenses," the physician said.

"Lenses?" King Charming asked.

"Yes, Your Majesty. Lenses to be worn over the eyes."

"Are you talking about *glasses?*" King Charming leaped to his feet again. "No son of mine is going to be called Four Eyes!"

"Glasses?" the queen asked. "But those are so unbecoming. Surely there's another solution. No Charming has ever worn glasses."

"But these are not ordinary glasses. Of course not, Your Majesties. These are *special* glasses, required for *overly* perfect vision."

Both the king and queen looked pleased. "*Special* glasses are acceptable."

And so it was that Dexter became the first Charming to wear glasses. They'd become as much a part of him as his arms and legs. They'd enhanced his life. But now, with a jousting tournament on the horizon, the glasses were proving to be an impediment.

He plucked another buttercup from the field. "The helmet is standard issue. I have to wear it," he told

Darling. "But the faceplate wasn't designed for glasses. And you know I can't wear contacts." It was true. Dexter's eyes were so sensitive, if a speck of dust or stray eyelash got into one of them, it could only be removed by a puff of fairy breath. It was quite an ordeal.

"Why not have a new helmet designed to fit over your glasses?" Darling suggested. She'd had her workout suit tailored for her exact measurements. "Then it will fit you perfectly."

"That's impossible. Parents Weekend is in a few days. There's not enough time." He sneezed again.

Darling pursed her lips. She'd long ago learned an important lesson—there was always a way to wrestle with the impossible. If not allowed to climb in public, simply climb when everyone else is asleep. If not allowed to gallop, then pretend your horse took you off course and gallop as soon as you're out of sight.

And if something doesn't fit, mold it to your own specifications.

As she wondered who might be able to help with such short notice, Dexter slowly got to his feet. "I'm so glad Mom and Dad aren't coming. It's going to be bad enough having all the other parents watch me fall off my horse." He brushed a few blades of grass off his chain mail tunic.

Darling's MirrorPhone buzzed. "Uh-oh," she said as she scrambled to her feet. "It's a group hext from Mom." She showed the screen to Dexter, and they groaned at the same time.

Dearest Charming children,
We have rescheduled our Mermaid cruise.
See you on Parents Weekend.

"And I thought the day couldn't get any worse," Dexter said. "Why can't I be in a chess match for Parents Weekend? Or a gaming competition? I'm good at those things. Why do we even have to joust? The only people who joust these days are those weird old knights from Wonderland…or people who get summer jobs in theme parks."

"We could trade," she said with a devious smile. "I'll joust, and you'll go to Damsel-In-Distressing."

He smiled back. "Mom would faint if she heard you say that."

They shared a laugh. Then Darling straightened her skirt and rearranged her tiara. "Since Mom and Dad are coming for Parents Weekend, we'll have to be on our best Charming behavior, and that means you have to get ready for this joust." She picked up her brother's helmet. "Let's go get this fixed."

Chapter

7

The Village

Smithy

The Village of Book End was a short walk from campus. Dexter found that it was easier to wear the suit of armor than to carry all the pieces, even if it meant extra sneezes. But Darling insisted on holding the helmet. She liked the feel of the metal in her hands. If she'd had a moment to herself, she would have slipped it over her head. But that would be very unbecoming for a Charming princess. Besides, the helmet wasn't designed to fit over a tiara any more than it was designed to fit over glasses.

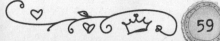

Book End was a quaint village, set along a cobbled, meandering street. Some shops, such as the Mad Hatter of Wonderland's Haberdashery & Tea Shoppe and the Beanstalk Bakery, looked as if they'd come straight out of a storybook, while others, like the Glass Slipper Shoe Store and the Hocus Latte Café, had a much more modern appeal. Though a walk to the village was a welcome break from school, Darling didn't go very often. While many of the boys on the school campus had grown used to seeing her and had learned she wasn't going to marry any of them, she was still a novelty to many of the local village boys.

"Here we go," Dexter said sarcastically as a boy stuck his head out of the Red Shoes Dance Club.

"I love your family!" he cried, a woozy look spreading across his face.

"Don't worry," Darling called. "You'll get over it." She'd been thinking about ordering cards with that phrase so she could hand them out as needed. Another boy ran out of the bakery and thrust a slice of

red-velvet cheesecake at her. "For you, Charming princess! Will you marry me?"

Dexter stepped protectively between his sister and the panting boy. "My sister isn't marrying anyone. And she's not eating that—she's lactose-intolerant!" he said. The lactose part wasn't true, but it was a polite way to get rid of the boy.

They walked a few more paces, then Dexter came to an abrupt stop. Darling assumed he was about to protect her from another suitor, but his gaze was fixed on a girl. She was at a coffee stand, ordering a drink. Her black hair was pulled into a long braid, and her purple boots were laced up to her knees. "Raven," Dexter whispered.

Raven Queen, daughter of the infamous Evil Queen, was one of the best-known students on campus, not only because of her lineage but also because she was credited with having started the whole "Rebel" trend. She'd refused to sign the Storybook of Legends and had torn out her page, which meant that she'd refused to accept and commit herself to her prewritten destiny. She also began to publicly question her destiny. Some of the students respected her, but others were critical.

Darling thought Raven was courageous.

And Dexter clearly thought she was much more than that. He looked as love-struck as the boy with the piece of cheesecake. "Dex?" Darling said. Raven had collected her drink and was sitting at a table with some other students. "Dex?"

"Huh?"

"You're staring."

"I am?" He gulped.

"Come on." She gave him a little push to get him walking again. "Of all the people to be crushing on, you choose the daughter of the Evil Queen." She shook her head and laughed.

"I know, I know," he said with a scowl. "Mom and Dad would royally freak out if they knew."

"Don't worry. Your secret's safe with me."

They turned down a narrow street. Dexter's

armored foot coverings, or sollerets, clanged on the cobblestones. Since neither of the Charming siblings had been to the blacksmith's shop, they asked for directions from a crooked man who was sitting on the stoop of his crooked house.

"See that trail of smoke?" he said, pointing to the end of the lane. "That's the place."

"Thanks," Dexter told him. "You okay carrying that?" he asked his sister for the zillionth time. "It's kind of heavy."

"I'm fine," she said. Unbeknownst to her brother, she could have carried the helmet all day and wouldn't have strained a single muscle, thanks to all those push-ups and chin-ups.

They reached the end of the lane and stood outside a warehouse-style building with red metal siding. A black chimney pipe stuck out of the silver metal roof. A thin tendril of smoke drifted from the pipe, gradually fading as it reached toward the sky. Silver vines grew up the sides of the building, but upon closer inspection, the vines turned out to be sculpted from sheets of aluminum. A bronze sign hung from the eave.

SMITHY

"I guess that's short for *blacksmith*," Darling said.

The front door was cast from metal, with inlaid flames decorating the panels. Dexter grabbed the wrought-iron handle. As they stepped inside, a hammering sound filled their ears.

The room was vast and filled with benches, power tools, and machinery stations. A brick hearth sat in the center of the room. A small flame flickered, glowing green, then blue—a sure sign that it had been born in a dragon's mouth. A workstation was set up next to the hearth. A woman sat there, perched on a tall stool. One of her hands held a pair of tongs, which gripped a red-hot piece of metal. The other hand held a huge hammer. She wore a

leather apron, protective goggles, and headphones. Her hammering reverberated throughout the room.

Darling plugged her ears as Dexter shouted, "Hello!" The woman didn't notice. "Hello!" Still, no reaction. Then he sneezed.

The woman looked up. She removed her headphones. "Yes?" she asked.

"Is the blacksmith here?" Dexter asked. "I need some work done."

The woman set her project aside, then stood. Both Darling and Dexter craned their necks as they looked up at her. She wasn't a giant, but she stood at least seven feet tall. Her hair hung in dozens of braids, each one as black as witch's ink. Flame tattoos covered her bare arms, and a diamond sparkled on her left nostril.

She slid her goggles onto her forehead. "I'm the smithy. Betty Bunyan's the name."

"Bunyan?" Darling asked. She glanced at a painting that hung on the wall. It was a portrait of a lumberjack who stood as tall as the trees surrounding him. He was dressed in a plaid shirt and dungarees, and he carried an ax over his shoulder. "You're Paul Bunyan's daughter?"

"Yep, that's dear old Dad," she said. Then she pointed to another painting, which was almost identical except the lumberjack was younger in appearance. "And that's my big brother, Paul Junior. Dad gave him an ax and taught him how to be a logger." Her expression suddenly clouded. "I wanted an ax, too, but Dad said it was too dangerous. He said logging wasn't for me." She stood in silence for a moment, staring at the painting. The dragon flame flickered, reflecting off the metal ceiling. Darling recognized the yearning in Betty's eyes.

"You could always buy yourself an ax," Darling said gently.

"Buy one?" Betty laughed. "I taught myself how to *make* one. And then I went my own way and opened this shop." She punched Darling in the shoulder. "A girl's gotta do what a girl's gotta do. Am I right?"

"I wouldn't really know about that," Darling said, trying to sound confused. Though she and Dexter were as close as peas in a pod, she still kept her workouts a secret from him. It wasn't because she was worried he'd judge her—he would never do that. It was mostly because she didn't want to put him in a position where he also had to keep a secret from their parents.

Betty pointed at Dexter's chest. "Hey, I recognize the Charming crest. You must be Daring's younger brother."

"Yes, I'm Dexter, and this is my sister, Darling." He shook the smithy's hand. Darling tucked the helmet under her left arm, then held out her right hand.

"I didn't know there was a sister," Betty said as she shook Darling's hand. Her grip was strong. "How come I've never heard of you?"

Darling shrugged. "Charming girls aren't as well known as Charming boys. According to my story, I'm not supposed to be a hero like my brothers. My destiny is to be rescued. Basically, that means I'm not supposed to do much but wait around."

Betty turned Darling's hand over, exposing the palm. "You've got calluses," she said. "That's not the sign of a girl who's been waiting around."

Darling slid from Betty's grip, then hid her hands behind her back. The calluses had come from climbing. No matter how much lotion she used, they wouldn't go away. Darling gulped. She wasn't sure what to say.

Betty's gaze traveled between brother and sister. Then, as she looked at Darling once more, her gaze filled with understanding. "My mistake," Betty said. "It's my hands that have the calluses. Yours are as soft as a princess's hands should be." She turned back to Dexter. "Looks like you got banged up a bit. Whatcha been doing?"

"It's my first day in armor," he explained.

"Your first day?" She laughed. "You got that many dents and dings on your first day? I've never seen a dent on your brother's armor. He brings it in once a week for a buff and polish. It's always perfect. Not a scratch."

Dexter looked down at the floor. Once again, he was being reminded of his brother's superiority. Darling could practically feel his pain. "Dex is just as strong and able as Dare."

"No, I'm not," he said.

"Yes, you are," Darling retorted. "Only you're strong in other areas. You always help me with crownloading new apps, and you always help tutor Daring in Crownculus."

Dexter lowered his gaze. "Gee, thanks, Darling."

"But this has nothing to do with strength or intelligence," Darling said. "Dex's armor is dented because he can't see where he's going. His faceplate won't fit over his glasses."

Betty examined the helmet. "These old-fashioned helmets weren't designed for glasses. I'd have to make a brand-new one for you."

"That would be great," Dexter said. "I need it right away. I'm supposed to be in a jousting tournament this weekend."

"I can't make you a new helmet that quickly." She pointed to her workstation. "I've got a big order of MirrorPhone covers for the Ever After High Bookstore." The covers were scattered across a worktable. Each bore the initials EAH. "But I can probably get out those dents and give the suit a good polish. Go ahead and leave it on that bench. You can pick it up tomorrow."

"Okay," Dexter said with a sigh. He adjusted his glasses, then wandered over to the bench and began removing the armor. He looked deflated, as if he'd already failed the tournament. As if he could already see King Charming's disappointed face.

Darling chewed on her lower lip. MirrorPhone covers were definitely not as important as her brother's sense of pride. She motioned Betty aside, then spoke in a lowered voice. "If my brother Dare were standing here, asking you to make a new helmet, would you find time for him?" Betty didn't answer, but she suddenly looked guilty. "Dex wants the opportunity to prove to everyone that he's just as good as Dare. That he's a champion, too."

Betty glanced over at the portrait of Paul Junior. Then she looked down at Darling. "What about you?"

"What about me?"

"Do you want the same opportunity that's been given to your brothers?" she asked.

Darling suddenly felt as if she could trust this woman. Betty hadn't been given an ax, so she'd gone out and made one. She wasn't the sort of person to sit around and wait. "Of course," Darling replied. "With all my heart."

Betty Bunyan narrowed her eyes. Then she smiled. "Hey, Dexter."

"Yes?" He was standing in a T-shirt and shorts, the armor piled on the bench.

"I'll do my best to make that helmet for you. Come by tomorrow morning."

Dexter beamed. "Thanks!"

Darling smiled at Betty. She knew in her heart that she'd found a kindred spirit.

The Stress of Being Distressed

When they reached campus, Dexter hurried off to a Tech Club meeting. His Ever After High friends didn't care if he could or couldn't joust. They appreciated his nerdy side. While Darling had friends at school, she was too guarded to let anyone know about her rebellious side. Even Dexter didn't know her entire story, and he was pretty much her best friend. Maybe one day she could be open with the world— including her parents. She could tell them that she longed to run in a marathon, or to join a mountain-climbing expedition. To be a hero and come to someone's rescue. What a grand day that would be!

But today was not that day. So Darling grabbed a quick lunch in the Castleteria with her friends Cerise Hood and Cedar Wood, then hurried to the Damsel-In-Distressing classroom.

The room was lushly decorated, as befits a damsel. Instead of desks with straight-backed chairs, velvet sofas were provided, allowing the girls to drape themselves like limp noodles, rendering the illusion of utter helplessness. Chandeliers supplied soft lighting, so no harsh shadows would fall upon their lovely faces. And three of the walls were mirrored, so appearances could be checked at all times. The room looked as it had for generations, but recently, high-tech gadgets had been added into the nooks and crannies. For example, with a voice command, the room's temperature could instantly turn steamy hot to mimic a dragon's den, or icy cold to mimic a mountain tower. It was important to practice being

distressed in a variety of climates. With a push of a button, screens would drop from the wall, creating various landscapes where a damsel might find herself. Props and sound effects were also available.

Out in the hallway, Darling accepted a note from a grinning boy who had drawn up a list of reasons why he was the perfect choice to marry into the Charming family. Then she glided into the classroom. Duchess Swan, daughter of the Swan Queen, had already arrived. She was dressed in her usual ballet tutu and tights. She glanced at the note in Darling's hand.

"Another proposal?" Duchess said with a slight sneer. "How proud you must be that all the boys want to marry you." Her sarcasm was as thick as pond scum.

"You know it's not like that," Darling said as she tucked the note into a pocket.

"How would I know what it's like?" Duchess said, adjusting her strand of pearls. "I wasn't born into a family that gets everything it wants."

Not everything, Darling thought. But she didn't blame Duchess for her bitterness. The poor girl was doomed to spend her life as a swan, waiting for a rescue that, according to her story, would never come.

A few moments later, all the students had arrived. They'd been chosen for the class because their stories destined them to need rescuing. The girls varied from those who wouldn't have it too bad to those whose situations would be life-threatening. In the nondangerous category was Holly O'Hair, Rapunzel's daughter, who'd be stuck in a tower. And Ashlynn Ella, daughter of Cinderella, who'd be stuck in servitude to a wicked stepmother and stepsisters. In the more dangerous category, there was Briar Beauty, daughter of Sleeping Beauty, who'd fall into a deep slumber. And Apple, who'd eat a poisoned apple and fall into a coma. In the most horrid category, there was Cerise Hood, daughter of Red Riding Hood, who'd be devoured by a big, bad wolf! And then there were the two oddballs—Duchess, who expected no rescuer, and Darling, who would be rescued, but from *what* she didn't yet know.

As the girls helped themselves to iced mint tea and miniature thronecakes, Headmaster Grimm strode into the classroom. "Greetings, students," he said. "Please settle down, for I have an announcement to make." It wasn't unusual for the headmaster to pop into class for a quick visit, but his expression was dour and his tone more serious than usual.

The girls sat down and waited while the headmaster cleared his throat. "Most of you took Damsel-In-Distressing last quarter, and your instructor was Madam Maid Marian. With Parents Weekend just around the corner, I had hoped to bring in a very special guest teacher this quarter. Lady Helen of Troy had agreed to travel to Ever After High to help prepare you for your presentation to the parents. But, alas, she's been asked to launch a new fleet of ships and will not be available."

Only Apple groaned. Everyone else looked bored. Briar had fallen asleep, so Apple gently woke her.

"I am equally disappointed. Lady Helen is the epitome of a distressed damsel and would have been an excellent role model for you. Having been kidnapped as a young lady, she knows firsthand what it is like to wait for rescue." He smoothed his waistcoat. "But we'll just have to make the best of the situation. Please welcome your teacher." All eyes turned toward the doorway.

In stepped a woman wearing a cone hat and veil.

Darling smiled. Of all the instructors she'd had last quarter, Madam Maid Marian had been her favorite.

"Thank you, Headmaster Grimm," Madam Maid Marian said. "Your warm introduction brought tears to my eyes." The sarcasm was undeniable.

One of Darling's favorite books was Marian's autobiography, *Secrets of the Sherwood Forest*. She'd read it a dozen times and kept it hidden in her tiara trunk. Madam Maid Marian was an inspiration. Though she'd begun her life as a damsel, pampered and spoiled, she'd fallen in love with a renegade named

Robin Hood and had joined his band of roving thieves. So hexciting!

Headmaster Grimm pulled Madam Maid Marian aside. He spoke to her in a hushed tone, but his voice was naturally loud, so all the students could clearly hear the conversation. "Madam Maid Marian, I do hope that you will focus on your experiences as a damsel, rather than on your years as a…"

"A Rebel?" she asked innocently.

"We do not use that term around here," he said. "But, yes, that is my point. Last quarter, you had the students escape from the tower on their own, rather than wait for rescue. That was not approved curriculum. You are teaching *damsels*, not delinquents."

"I understand." Was that a touch of scorn in her voice? The veil hid Madam Maid Marian's face, so Darling couldn't see her expression.

"It is important that you prepare the young ladies for Parents Weekend. Each class will be asked to give a presentation."

"Of course."

Headmaster Grimm nodded. Then he turned back to the students. "Carry on, girls." And with crisp footsteps, he left the classroom.

Madam Maid Marian set a black bag under the desk, then removed her cone hat. Her hair was chestnut and cut in a short bob. She was fresh-faced, with no makeup. A few freckles dotted her wide nose and high cheekbones. She wore the colors of the forest, with a moss-green tunic and brown leggings. A pair of green feather earrings completed the woodsy look. Her suede boots looked super comfortable.

"Hi," she said. "It's nice to see all of you again." She sat on the edge of the desk. "I wasn't sure I'd be teaching again, so I'm afraid I'm a bit unprepared. Does anyone know what we're supposed to be doing today?"

Apple's hand shot up. "We need to be graded on our waiting thronework."

"Waiting?"

"We were supposed to practice waiting," Briar explained. "You know, to be rescued."

"You've got to be kidding." Did Madam Maid Marian just roll her eyes? Darling sat up straighter. She couldn't believe it. The teacher seemed to have a bit of an attitude.

"We're not kidding," Apple said. "Waiting was our thronework."

Ashlynn sipped her mint tea. "I hope we don't have to do it again. I felt silly just sitting there."

"Me too," said Cerise.

"I don't know why you're complaining," Duchess said with a definite eye roll. "I'm so totally stressed out. What with my other classes and ballet practice, waiting is a welcome relief. Besides, at least you're waiting for a reason. You all get rescued." She shoved a whole thronecake into her mouth and chewed in a quick, frustrated way.

Darling watched quietly. She was not one to readily offer her opinions. Like Dexter, she took her time observing and was very calculated when she finally spoke in public. Which is why she was startled when Madam Maid Marian looked right at her and asked, "What do you think, Ms. Charming?"

"Well…" She fiddled with her dress sleeves. "I think…" She paused. "I think that if you are going to be a traditional damsel in distress, then learning how to wait is a good idea." Apple nodded in agreement.

Madam Maid Marian smiled. "Very wisely put." Then she waved her hand through the air. "I declare that you all pass your waiting thronework. What's next?"

Holly pressed a button on her MirrorPad. "It says in our syllabus that we're supposed to work on sound recognition today." Then she read the instructions out loud:

Class: Damsel-In-Distressing

Lesson: Sound Recognition, Part One
While waiting for rescue, the damsel must be alert to all sorts of sounds. Some are of no concern,

some warn of danger, while others mean imminent rescue. If the damsel is untrained, she may ignore an important sound and not be prepared for rescue. Or worse—she might miss out on the rescue and never get her Happily Ever After.

Instructions: Load the cassette tape labeled SOUND RECOGNITION, PART ONE into the classroom's sound system. Follow the directions.

"Cassette tape?" Cerise said with a laugh. "What the hex is that? This lesson must be ancient."

Madam Maid Marian found the tape in the desk drawer. Apple gently woke Briar so she wouldn't miss the lesson. The girls grabbed more tea and settled on the velvet cushions. Darling wondered if she could order a pair of Marian's suede boots on the Mirror Network. They looked as though they'd be good for climbing.

"Welcome to Damsel-In-Distressing Sound Recognition Lesson, Part One," the cassette tape's narrator said. "You will hear a sound. You will have a few moments to guess the sound's origin before the correct answer is revealed. The first sound is…"

Galloping filled the speakers, faint at first, then increasing in volume.

"Oh, that's easy," Apple said. "That's Daring Charming coming to my rescue."

"Or someone else," Duchess said. "It's not written in stone that Daring will be *your* Prince Charming. He might be someone else's." It was well known that Duchess had a crush on Daring.

"You are mistaken," Apple said with polite certainty. "Of course he's going to be *my* Prince Charming. I even had key chains made commemorating our future marriage."

Duchess looked like she was about to say something else, but the narrator interrupted. "That was the sound of the rescuing prince making his approach," the narrator said. "This is an extremely important sound because it gives the damsel fair warning that she should make herself presentable. After a damsel is locked in a tower or dungeon, her hair will surely be a mess."

"Yeah, and her mind will be a mess, too," Holly murmured.

The narrator continued. "The second sound is…" Beating wings filled the speakers.

"That's a dragon," Ashlynn said. "Or it could be a griffin. But since griffins don't normally kidnap damsels, I'm guessing dragon. And to beat that kind of rhythm, you'd need a wingspan of at least twenty feet across." Ashlynn was considered a bit of an animal expert on campus. She spoke many different animal languages, including Squirrel Squeak and Griffinglish.

"If you are destined to be held captive by a dragon," the narrator said, "this is the sound you will hear before the dragon carries you away. Upon hearing this sound, it is suggested that you quickly pack items into a purse or pocket. A hairbrush, lip gloss, and moist towelettes will help keep your face fresh for when the prince arrives."

"I'd grab a book," Apple said.

"I'd get my music," Briar said.

"I'd take my cloak," Cerise said.

"I'd take a sword." Darling's hand flew to her mouth. She hadn't meant to say that.

Madam Maid Marian leaned forward, her eyebrows raised. "And why would you take a sword, Ms. Charming?"

Everyone stared at her. Madam Maid Marian nodded encouragingly. "Because I'd want to protect myself," Darling said with a sudden rush of confidence.

"I don't think a sword is the right answer," Apple pointed out. "I mean, if we had swords, we wouldn't need to be rescued. And then we wouldn't need to take this class."

Duchess snorted. "That sounds like something a Rebel would say."

The narrator cleared her throat, as if trying to get the class's attention. "The final sound of the day is sound number three." They waited, but nothing came out of the speakers.

"It must not be working," Briar said.

"Sound number three was the sound of waiting," the tape's narrator said. "Waiting is an important sound that the damsel must get used to."

"That wasn't the sound of waiting," Madam Maid Marian said with a shake of her head. "That was the sound of life passing you by."

Gallant

Sir Gallopad

That evening's curfew check was assigned to Mrs. Her Majesty the White Queen. Being from Wonderland, she tended to do things in a Wonderlandian sort of way. That was why, when she stuck her head into Darling and Rosabella's room to see if the girls were tucked snugly in bed, she said, "Good night, good night, and if the bedbugs should bite, biting them back would be a delight." Then she slammed the door shut and marched off to the next room.

Darling lay as still as possible, waiting until Rosabella's breathing had slowed and deepened. Soft snoring drifted from a floral bouquet, where Adelita the butterfly was sleeping on a rose petal bed. Darling glanced at the clock. Time was running out. It was now or never.

Moving like a shadow, she stuffed pillows beneath her silk quilt so it would look as if she were still in bed. Honestly, she probably could have stomped around and Rosabella wouldn't have woken up. The girl was always so exhausted after her full days of taking classes, leading peaceful protests, and collecting signatures for various petitions that she fell asleep as soon as her head hit the pillow. Darling tiptoed into the bathroom, where she changed out of her nightgown and into her workout suit. She added a matching jacket to combat the evening's chill, and a pair of running shoes. Once her hair was secured in a ponytail, she crept onto the balcony, then climbed down the vines until she was safely on the ground.

If she was caught breaking curfew, there'd be a phone call to her parents. Which would lead to a big lecture. There'd be no way to explain her motives. Charming princesses didn't sneak out at night. They didn't seek adventure. And they certainly didn't break rules.

But when Madam Maid Marian had said that the sound of waiting was actually the sound of life passing by, Darling had wanted to leap to her feet and hug her. It was as if she had looked right into Darling's soul and had read those words etched on her heart.

The night air was crisp and refreshing. The moon had not yet risen, but the campus was well lit. If she jumped into the Ever After High wishing well, she'd land in the mountains beyond the Dark Forest, but she didn't want to travel that far. She had one destination in mind, and to get there, she planned on traveling in a very traditional way.

A *clip-clop* sound neared. Headmaster Grimm was serious about security, which was why he'd hired All the King's Horses and All the King's Men to patrol the grounds after dark. Darling darted behind a bush as a pair rode past. The horses snorted but didn't notice her. Nor did the soldiers, who were chatting about some sort of sporting match they'd watched on the Mirror Network. As soon as the coast was clear, Darling ran all the way to the stables.

Most of the students at Ever After High had pets. Some had brought their creatures from home, while others had received theirs in a special ceremony in the Enchanted Forest. Sir Gallopad, a pure-white horse with a glossy white mane, had been chosen for Darling specifically for his size and demeanor. He was small, shy, and quiet. He'd never thrown anyone from the saddle, had never bucked or kicked. Riding him could be a chore because he liked to stop and nibble on shrubbery. The Charming Committee on Appropriate Pets had been delighted with Sir Gallopad, confident that the princess would be safe with such a timid creature. And they were thrilled to learn that he possessed the magical ability to change colors, which allowed him to camouflage himself if danger should appear. But what the committee didn't know was that, like Darling, Sir Gallopad also had a secret.

He loved to gallop!

She crept past the stalls that housed some of the other pets, including Briar Beauty's Divacorn and C.A. Cupid's Pegasus. "Hi," she whispered as she opened the last stall. To the untrained eye, it would have appeared that Darling was speaking to a huge mound of straw. But in an instant, the mound changed color, revealing a small white horse. Sir Gallopad was wide awake, as if he'd sensed that she was on her way. She scratched between his ears. "Want to go for a ride?" He smiled at her and nuzzled her cheek. Then she slipped the reins over his head and led him outside. No saddle was necessary. With ease, she lifted herself onto his back and then gently urged him toward the campus boundary.

Because a number of students had been caught sneaking into the Village of Book End after hours and frolicking in the Enchanted Forest when they

were supposed to be in bed, Headmaster Grimm had installed an additional security measure. Every night, at the twelfth stroke of midnight, a one-hundred-foot-tall wall of briars appeared along the campus perimeter, so thick and thorny that no one could pass through unless they knew the security code. And every morning, with the first ray of dawn, the briars disappeared, as if they'd never existed. The trick for any wandering student was to leave campus before the briars grew, then return at dawn and sneak back into the dormitory without anyone noticing.

Dong.

Uh-oh. She glanced over at the clock tower. It was the first stroke of midnight.

"Hurry," she told Sir Gallopad. At the edge of campus, the ground cracked open and briar tips poked out of the earth. *Dong.* They grew a foot. She'd never ridden through the thorny shrubbery. It was risky, but if they galloped at full speed, they might make it before the thorns fully sprouted.

"Halt!" a voice called.

Sir Gallopad skidded to a stop and immediately turned the color of the nearby stone wall. One of the King's Men approached. His black stallion had fierce eyebrows and flared nostrils.

"Who goes there?" the soldier demanded. Darling clenched her jaw. To be discovered outside after curfew would greatly disappoint her parents—but worse, she wasn't dressed properly, and she'd never hear the end of that.

So, just as the soldier rode up to her, she untied her ponytail and flipped her hair. This wasn't because she'd found a bug in it, or because she was trying to look even more charming. It was how she activated her secret enchantment—a secret she kept to herself and used only in dire emergencies. Getting caught in a workout suit after curfew seemed to fit that category.

With a dramatic flip of her silky locks, Darling could slow time, almost to the point of making it stand still. It lasted only a few moments, but it was long enough for Darling and Sir Gallopad to escape through the briars, which still had wide spaces between them. Once she'd crossed the campus border, she turned and watched as time returned to normal. The soldier scratched his head in puzzlement. All he knew was that a girl had vanished into thin air. *Dong.* The briars rose to their full one-hundred-foot height, and Darling was safe from view.

Freedom! She rode across the footbridge, through the meadow, and into the Enchanted Forest. Moonlight trickled between leaves, and a pair of wide eyes blinked from a nearby tree. Sir Gallopad didn't startle at the sound of an owl or the rustling of branches. He was as brave as any of the King's Horses. Excitement darted up Darling's spine. She gripped the reins and tightened her legs. Then she leaned close to Sir Gallopad's ear and whispered, "Go."

There was no sensation like galloping. Sir Gallopad wove between trees and leaped over fallen logs. It was an obstacle course fit for a professional team, but Darling and Sir Gallopad were naturals. Their instincts blended, taking cues from each other.

Together, the shy horse and the quiet princess were a force with which to be reckoned.

When they'd both reached exhaustion and the midnight ride was over, they stopped at a stream for water. Because of the security system, there was no way to get back to school until dawn, so Sir Gallopad lay on the mossy forest floor. Darling settled next to him, resting her head on his warm back. As her eyelids grew heavy, she smiled. There had been no one to tell her that galloping was too dangerous. No one tossing bouquets or hollering marriage proposals. That night she'd been free of all that, and she'd felt completely at ease. As the owl hooted softly, bidding them good night, Darling closed her eyes and fell into the deep sleep that comes with happiness.

Just before dawn, Darling's MirrorPhone alarm chimed. She brushed fallen leaves from her face. "Time to get back," she told Sir Gallopad. He snorted, his breath misty in the cool air. As she started to rise, Darling found a small arrow lying on the ground at her feet. "Where'd this come from?" she asked. The arrow's shaft was made from pale birch wood. Green feathers were bound to its end with a thin leather cord. "These are just like the feathers that Madam Maid Marian wore in her earrings," Darling said, holding the arrow out so Sir Gallopad could sniff it. His ears flicked. The MirrorPhone alarm chimed a second time. There was no time to ponder the arrow's appearance. Best to leave it where it had been found, in case someone came looking. Darling swung her leg up and over Sir Gallopad's back. He carried her swiftly across the bridge and to the wall of briars.

As the first ray of dawn appeared, the briars and their deadly barbs evaporated. The cracks in the ground sealed, and grass sprouted in their place. The King's Men watered and fed their horses, then marched back to their barracks for a meal and sleep. As soon as they'd closed the barracks door, Darling rode into the stables. It was the stable ogre's duty to feed the pets, but he wouldn't arrive until breakfast time, so she gave Sir Gallopad an extra handful of oats. She kissed him on the muzzle, then nimbly made her way back to the dormitory and climbed the vines to her room. Rosabella stirred briefly, complained that it was too early to wake up, then rolled onto her stomach. Darling put on her nightgown, hid the workout suit and sneakers in the back of her closet, and slipped into bed.

Even though she had an hour to catch a few more winks, her eyes were wide open. The arrow hadn't been in the forest when she'd fallen asleep. Whoever owned it must have been out past curfew.

Perhaps Darling wasn't the only person at Ever After High who had secrets.

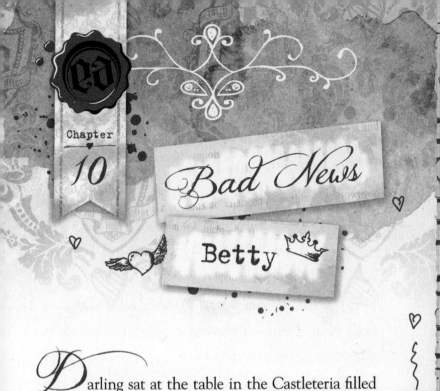

Bad News

Betty

$\mathcal{D}$arling sat at the table in the Castleteria filled with classic princesses, eating their late breakfasts. The table wasn't reserved for students of royal heritage only, but the girls tended to stick together.

"Blech," Briar complained as she stirred her porridge. "Why is Hagatha's porridge always lumpy?" Hagatha was in charge of the Castleteria kitchen. A rather hairy old lady, she tended to cook bland, traditional foods. She'd never been nominated for chef of the year.

 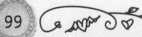

"Hagatha adds the lumps on purpose," Apple said. "Literally." Sure enough, a box labeled LUMPS sat on a shelf in the Castleteria's pantry.

"We shouldn't be worried about lumps," Rosabella said. "We should be worried about the fact that the porridge is made from magically modified grains."

"Lay it on us," Briar said with an eye roll. "It's not as if we were enjoying this anyway."

"Magically modified food is a serious issue," Rosabella said. "We don't know the long-term effects on our bodies." She grabbed her ever-present picket sign. "I'm going to protest. Who's with me?"

All the girls suddenly checked their MirrorPhones as if an important hext had arrived.

"Suit yourselves," she said. "I'm going to talk to Ginger Breadhouse. She's the best cook on campus. Surely she cares about this issue." She hurried over to the next table.

"Good luck," Darling called. Rosabella's protests were important, but there were *so* many things she wanted to change. It was exhausting after a while.

A bell chimed and Headmaster Grimm appeared on the Castleteria's large mirror screen. The headmaster was seated behind his heavy oak desk. Even though he wasn't royalty, his chair resembled a throne. "Good morning, students. Today's weather forecast calls for an agreeable amount of sunshine with intermittent spells of pleasantness. This evening, however, winds are expected out of the north, which might bring a batch of flying badgers. But not to worry—the weather should be perfect for Parents Weekend." The camera moved into an extreme close-up of his face. His bushy eyebrows furrowed. "I am reminding each and every one of you that your best behavior is expected for Parents Weekend. Rebellious activity of any sort will not be tolerated." His eyeballs moved to the left of the screen and stared down at the exact spot where Raven Queen was sitting.

"What?" Raven said with a shrug. "I'm just eating my breakfast. Yeesh."

The camera widened to a shot of the headmaster at his desk. "Parents Weekend is one of our most important events at Ever After High, and I have full confidence that each of you will make your parents proud. However, if anyone hears of rebellious plans being made, report them immediately to my office." The screen went black.

"Parents Weekend is a royal pain," Briar said. "The cleaning fairies are already fully booked. I'm going to have to clean my room myself."

"I can give you the number of a great cleaning dwarf service," Apple said. "They sing the cutest songs while they work."

"That would be hexcellent," Briar said.

"Don't clean my side of the room," Ashlynn said. She and Briar were roommates. "My mom would flip her crown if she found out I didn't do it myself! The whole Cinderella story starts out with cleaning and scrubbing, you know."

Darling wasn't worried about her room. Even though she'd offered to do the work herself, her parents paid for a weekly cleaning fairy visit, which included laundry service. Unlike Ashlynn, Darling wasn't expected to engage in manual labor. "Does anyone know what kind of presentation Madam Maid Marian is planning for Parents Weekend?" she wondered.

Apple glanced up and down the table, then lowered her voice. "Headmaster Grimm did not seem pleased that Madam Maid Marian was teaching the class again. My parents are worried, too. They think she might influence us in a rebellious way." She shrugged. "Just because she went off story, that doesn't mean we'll go astray."

Silence descended over their small group, along with a guilty look on each of their faces. They'd all strayed from their stories in one way or another. Ashlynn was dating Hunter, who was a non-Royal, and Apple had openly supported their relationship. Briar had developed an interest in HeXtreme sports. And then there was Darling.

"Where are the boys?" Darling asked, hoping to change the subject.

"They left early to get ready for Hero Training class," Ashlynn explained. "Hunter looks so dreamy in his armor."

As the girls launched into a debate over which prince wore his armor best, Darling's MirrorPhone rang. It was Dexter. She excused herself from the table, then walked outside so she could hear better. "Hi," she said.

"I'm not allergic to armor after all," he told her, his voice ragged. "I'm actually sick. I can't go to classes today."

"For real?"

"Yes, for real." He sounded annoyed. "You think I'd fake being sick just to get out of jousting?"

"Of course not," she said, though she had considered that possibility. "What do you have?"

"I don't know. I'm at the infirmary right now, waiting to see the doctor. I've got a fever, and spots in my throat. And I'm blowing blue stuff out of my nose."

"Gross." She cringed. Then she added, "Sorry. Do you need anything?"

"No, just don't tell Mom. You know how she gets."

Dexter was right. Being sick was a very big deal in the Charming household. Charmings were supposed to have exceptional immune systems. On the rare occasion that one of her children fell ill, the queen went into a tizzy. It wasn't so much that she was worried about her children being uncomfortable. It was the simple fact that sickness marred their perfection. Inflamed runny noses, chapped lips, and bloodshot eyes should never be seen on a Charming face, thus as kids they were kept in the castle's nursery until all symptoms had cleared. When asked why a specific child hadn't been seen in a few days, the queen would say that the child had been sent to visit relatives. Never, ever would the Charming name be associated with nausea, chills, or flatulence.

"What am I going to do? If I can't practice, I'll make a fool of myself at the tournament."

"Don't talk like that," Darling said. Sometimes she couldn't understand her brother's lack of confidence. "You know you'll recover quickly. We Charmings

are never sick for long. I'm sure you'll be better by tonight."

"Yeah, probably."

"I don't have Damsel-In-Distressing until this afternoon. Can I do anything for you?"

"Yes. Keep this a secret, okay? Don't tell anyone I'm sick. I'll call you after I see the doctor."

"Okay. Bye."

Keeping the secret was easy. But Darling realized there was something else she could do. She could have Dexter's suit of armor and his new helmet delivered to his room. Then he wouldn't have to traipse into the village with a fever and runny nose. But when she dialed the number for the Smithy, there was no answer. "Hmmm," she said. "Betty must be hammering so loudly she can't hear the phone." So Darling decided to get the armor herself. It would be a nice surprise for Dexter. And it was a great excuse to stretch her legs, which were a bit sore from last night's ride.

As she walked down the lane toward the village, the usual chaos erupted when boys outside the walls of Ever After High caught their first glimpse of the one and only daughter of the Charming family. A majority of the boys couldn't keep up with Darling's pace—she could glide faster than most boys could walk.

Humphrey Dumpty, son of Humpty Dumpty, was sitting on a wall, and even though he'd seen Darling countless times, he grinned goofily, waved, then tumbled backward. "I'm okay," he hollered. "No cracks."

"Sorry," she called. But was it really her fault? Seriously, the son of Humpty Dumpty should *never* sit on a wall.

Before reaching the blacksmith's shop, she also caused a wagon collision, a small fire, and two concussions. "Unbelievable," she said with a shake of her head.

No smoke drifted from the smithy's chimney. The windows were dark. She grabbed the handle and pulled the door open. "Hello?" she called as she stepped inside. No hammering sounded. The room appeared to be empty. The dragon flame, now shrunk to the size of a baby's fingernail, was contained beneath a glass dome. "Hello?" she called again. Betty Bunyan was nowhere to be seen.

Dexter's armor was in the exact place he'd left it. The pieces were still covered in dents and dings. It hadn't been buffed or polished. Where was the new helmet that was supposed to fit over his glasses?

A piece of folded paper was tucked inside the old helmet.

Dear Dexter,

I got an emergency call from my dad.

He's in the hospital for bunion removal.

I'll be back in a few weeks, and I'll work on your armor then.

Betty B.

A few weeks? That would be way too late for Parents Weekend! Darling frowned. *Poor Dexter.* How could she break the bad news to him? He'd never succeed at jousting if he couldn't wear his glasses.

Darling sank onto the bench and sighed. It didn't matter what presentation Madam Maid Marian assigned to the Damsel-In-Distressing students, because Darling knew she'd be able to pull it off without a hitch. She'd appear to be the perfect Charming princess, and her parents would be none the wiser to her extracurricular activities. After all, she'd been faking her way through perfect princesshood for many years.

But Dexter couldn't fake perfect vision.

When the kids in spellementary school started calling Dexter "Four Eyes," King Charming had tried to cure his son of his overly perfect condition by turning to magic. He contacted every sorcerer in all the kingdoms, but the trouble with magical spells was that they all came with a hitch. *This spell will* turn you into a human, but, alas, you must give up your voice. This spell will allow you to dance the way you've always dreamed, but, alas, once you start dancing, you won't be able to stop. This spell will give you perfect eyesight, but, alas, you will look like a Cyclops.

Unless a miracle occurred, Dexter would have trouble during the jousting tournament. And fail in King Charming's eyes.

She reached for her phone to send Dexter a hext, but she decided it would be best to tell him in person. With or without a new helmet, he'd still need the armor for class tomorrow.

She started to pick up the pieces, then realized that the only way to carry them back to school would be to borrow one of Betty's carts. But pulling a cart through the village wasn't very princess-like. Sure, she could ask one of the Charming family fanboys to help, but that would mean enduring his yammering about her family and how she and he were meant for each other. *Gross!* She drummed a finger on her chin. *What if…?* No, she couldn't do that.

Could she?

Why not? Dexter was only an inch taller than she was, and he was definitely slender. She glanced around. The blacksmith's shop was empty.

No one would know.

Chapter

11

If the Suit

Fits

Darling removed her jewel-encrusted belt, then slipped out of her blue dress. Luckily, she wore a pair of metallic tights and a silver camisole underneath. She removed her ruffled heeled shoes, her necklace, and her tiara. Then she grabbed the chain mail tunic and slipped it over her head. It fell to her knees and hung loosely around her middle, but it was secure enough. She slipped her feet into the sollerets. Thankfully, Dexter's feet weren't much larger than hers. *This just might work!* On went the rest of the plate armor—

the shoulder pieces, breastplate, backplate, and thigh guards known as cuisses. The helmet was the most important part. A knight in dented armor wouldn't draw too much attention in town, but a princess in dented armor would. She braided her hair and tucked it into the helmet. It fit quite nicely.

She circled the shop's interior, beginning with slow, steady steps, then increasing her pace. The suit wasn't as heavy as she'd expected. She was amazed at how agile she felt, and how easily she could bend and jump. If Dexter got his new helmet, he'd have no problem riding a horse. She was sure of it. She found a pen and wrote on the back of Betty's note.

Dear Ms. Bunyan,
   I needed the armor for practice.
   Hope your father is feeling better.
   Please hext me when you return.
Thanks,
Dexter Charming

She included Dexter's phone number and set the note on the bench. Then she opened her Ever After High book bag, pushed her MirrorPad aside, and neatly packed her shoes, dress, necklace, and tiara. Realizing that her blue manicure might draw attention, she grabbed the gauntlets, slipped her hands inside, and then, bag in hand, strode from the blacksmith's shop.

It was quiet in the alley. Darling stood beneath the smithy's sign. *Am I really doing this?* she asked herself. She glanced down at her legs. *I'm completely covered. No one will know it's me. And lots of other students carry this same book bag.* She lowered the helmet's visor. Then, after a deep breath, she walked up the lane and turned onto Book End's Main Street.

The visor offered a strange, rectangular view of the world. But it was enough for her to walk safely and not bump into things. An odd sensation washed over her. Despite the fact that she was carrying extra weight, she felt lighter. No one ran after her with flowers or chocolates. No one fell to his knees to propose marriage. Her face was hidden, and no one knew who she was. No one could tell she was the Charming princess. For the first time in what felt like forever, Darling walked down the street in broad daylight and didn't cause a single ounce of chaos. A few people glanced her way, but nothing more. She usually hurried past the stores, trying to get out of the spotlight, but now she could actually take her time. She could even window-shop! What joy! She stopped at the Yarns & Noble Bookstore, where the latest volume of Diary of a Royal Kid was on display. The Glass Slipper Shoe Store's window featured platform shoes by the fashionable Shoemaker's Elves, and the Mad Hatter of Wonderland's Haberdashery & Tea Shoppe was having a two-for-one sale on jester hats.

"Hey, Dex!" a voice called.

Dex? Darling looked around. What was Dexter doing in Book End? He was supposed to be at the infirmary.

"Dex!" Daring strode toward her, a doughnut in hand. "Hey, did you see this? The Beanstalk Bakery named it after me. It's called Daring's Doughy

Delight." He smiled, nearly blinding a passerby. Then he stopped right in front of Darling and held the doughnut up to her visor. "It has three different kinds of icing and five different fillings. You can never have too many carbs." He flexed one of his arms.

Luckily, the slit in the visor wasn't big enough for Daring to notice it was his sister's eyes looking back at him. Or maybe he was too busy checking his reflection in the window to notice anything but his luxurious hair and chiseled jaw. "You want this?" he asked, offering her a piece. She shook her head, then watched as he ate it in two massive bites. He consumed food the way he consumed life—with gusto. "What are you doing out here? You're supposed to be practicing for the tournament."

Darling cringed, immediately regretting her impulsive decision to wear Dexter's armor. What was she supposed to do now? Daring took his role as her protective older brother very seriously. If he discovered that his little sister was walking around looking extremely untraditional, he'd give her a stern lecture.

"Your armor is a mess," he said. "You'd better take it to Betty for a buff and polish before Mom and Dad get here." Then he waved at a group of girls who were staring at him through the bookstore's window. Two of them fainted. Darling rolled her eyes. While she and Dexter shared similar quiet and unassuming dispositions, at least in public, she and Daring shared the same burden of being highly sought-after members of the Charming family. Daring, however, enjoyed his effect on the girls. He loved being the center of attention.

The girls who hadn't fainted rushed from the bookstore and began taking selfies with Daring. This was Darling's opportunity to escape. She hurried up the lane toward school. She'd leave the armor in Dexter's room, then continue with her normal schedule. "Hey, wait up!" Daring called. "I'll walk to class with you."

How could she get out of this? She couldn't show up at Hero Training! She'd have to tell Daring the truth.

"You'll be practicing with a lance today," Daring said. He'd been talking for a few minutes, but she'd

been so distracted by the situation that she hadn't been listening. "Of course, I don't need to practice. I'm the champion, after all. I can joust in my sleep. It just comes naturally, you know?"

Although her oldest brother sounded as though he was boasting, he really wasn't. Being good at everything was simply his reality. In the same way that she wasn't bragging when she said that most boys frequently tried to impress her in hopes of becoming the next Prince Charming. That was simply the annoying truth.

"Don't let yesterday get you down," he said with a slap on her back. "Sure, it was awkward when you fell off the horse, but it looks like you've gotten used to the armor. At least you're not falling over when you walk." He slapped her on the back again. She nearly coughed. "Just remember, Dad's going to be in the audience during the tournament. He'll be watching your every move."

Jeez, talk about pressure, Darling thought. *Poor Dex.*

"At least you don't have to win the tournament. You just have to be second best. That should be

118

easy. I'll be right here if you need help." He gave her a brotherly nudge, then settled into a lounge chair and began hexting on his MirrorPhone.

Here? Where was she? Daring had been talking so much she hadn't noticed that they'd turned off the lane. She lifted her visor so she could get a better look. Daring's chair was set at the edge of the field. Professor Knight was standing in the middle of the field, surrounded by a group of armor-clad students.

Uh-oh.

"Squire Charming!" the professor bellowed, pointing at her. "Thou art late!"

She had no idea what to do. If she turned and ran, Dexter would get in trouble for skipping class. The students might think he was scared. But she couldn't join them. Could she?

"Dexter!" Hunter Huntsman hurried to her side, his helmet tucked under an arm. She quickly flipped her visor over her face. "Hey, I wasn't sure if you'd make it. You were coughing pretty badly this morning. Are you feeling better?"

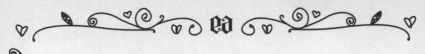

She shook her head.

"Squire Charming and Squire Huntsman!" Professor Knight bellowed. "Cease thy jibber-jabbering and attend within the instant or thou shalt be sent to the headmaster's office!"

"Guess it doesn't matter if you're sick," Hunter whispered. "You're stuck now." Hunter was Dexter's roommate, and they were an odd match. Hunter was tall, strapping, and athletic, fond of carrying an ax and walking around shirtless. He was the brawn to Dexter's brain. But they seemed to make it work. He grabbed the book bag from her hand and tossed it on the ground next to Daring. "Come on," he said.

Please oh please don't open that bag, Darling thought as she glanced at Daring. Then she followed Hunter onto the field.

Darling had never seen Professor Knight up close. She wasn't certain, but she guessed that he was the oldest teacher at Ever After High. His skin was as gray as Hagatha's porridge and as spotted as a witch's toadstool. The top of his head was mostly bald,

 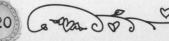

except for a few wisps of hair that appeared to be made of cloud. A long white beard hung to his belly. His suit of armor looked as if it had been left out in the rain for centuries. Each time he moved, bits of rust flaked off.

"On this day, thou shalt begin thy lessons in the art of jousting," he said, his voice surprisingly vibrant. "Jousting is the sport of heroes, born in the glorious days when chivalry reigned supreme."

Darling couldn't believe her ears. This was the kind of class she'd longed to take. They were going to learn something! *Do* something! She wanted to shout for joy!

"Whilst thou art destined to accomplish deeds of derring-do, exploits of extreme exceptionality, and acts of astounding achievement, not every hero is graced with the natural dexterity needed for a successful joust." Professor Knight looked straight at Darling. So did everyone else. "Alas, some of you will fail."

Fail? Is he seriously telling me that I don't have what it takes? she thought. Luckily the visor concealed her scowl. Then she remembered that everyone thought she was Dexter.

One of the students raised his hand. "Professor Knight? How come Daring is sitting over there?"

The professor scratched a clump of hair that was sprouting from his ear. "Squire Charming is observing today's lesson because he is our jousting champion. He hath no need to practice, for he is the perfect specimen of heroness." Daring glanced up for a moment, waved, then went back to hexting. "The knightly skills come naturally to Squire Charming, as they did to his father, of whom I had the honor to instruct. That was back in the day when knights were still appreciated. Your generation doesn't respect tradition, I'm afraid." He frowned. Darling fidgeted uneasily. At that moment, she was the perfect specimen of someone who was definitely not respecting tradition.

Professor Knight thrust a finger in the air. "Squires, it is time to mount your steeds."

Steeds? Darling's heart skipped a beat. This was getting better by the minute.

During the lecture, the horses had been brought up from the stables and were tied along a fence. There were a variety of horses to choose from. Hunter chose a horse that was stomping and straining against its tether. But Darling noticed the small, quiet horse who was nibbling on a patch of clover.

"Hello, Sir Gallopad," she whispered. His ears pricked, and he raised his head. He sniffed her, smiled, then licked her visor.

"Isn't that your sister's horse?" Hunter called. "You don't want that one. I hear he's super timid." Then he led his horse onto the field.

Darling looked around. The other students were distracted by their own horses. So she whispered again to Sir Gallopad. "I think we both need to stay hidden." And he immediately changed from white to black. "Good boy." She started walking and he followed.

This was going to be fun.

Princely

Pox

The door to Dexter and Hunter's room bore both the Charming family and the Huntsman family crests. Darling knocked as hard as she could. Since she was still wearing the gauntlets, the sound was astonishingly loud and echoed down the hall.

Her brother's voice, however, was quiet and hoarse. "Come in."

She threw open the door. "Dexter, I have the most amazing news," she cried, a bit out of breath. She'd run all the way to the dormitory, which hadn't been easy in the suit of armor. But she'd needed to get to the room before Hunter. "You won't believe it." She closed Dexter's door, tossed the book bag and gauntlets onto the faux-fur carpet, then whipped off the helmet.

Dexter was lying on his bed in his pajamas. His jackalope, a jackrabbit with antelope horns, Mr. Cottonhorn, was lying next to him, also in pajamas and wearing identical black-framed glasses. Dexter's mouth fell open. "Darling?" Mr. Cottonhorn dropped his book.

"Surprise," she said with a wide grin. Then her smile faded. "Oh, you look terrible." Dexter's nose was swollen and red, and little blue spots had sprouted all over his face. "What's the matter with you?"

He tried to sit up, but he fell back against the pillows with a groan. "Turns out I've got princely pox."

"What's that?"

"Apparently it's a form of pox that only princes can get. Most princes get it when they're babies, but lucky me, I'm getting it now." He sneezed. "Hunter doesn't have to worry about catching it, because he's not a prince."

She stepped closer to get a better view of the spots. "Do those things itch?"

"Uh-huh. The doctor said it'll take a few days before they go away and I feel better. I'm taking medicine, but it makes me really sleepy." He yawned and pointed to a bottle of prince pox potion. The label read: CAUSES DROWSINESS. DO NOT OPERATE ANY DRAWBRIDGES OR ENGAGE IN HEROIC ACTIVITIES WHILE TAKING THIS MEDICATION.

"A few days? Well, that means you might be well for the tournament. That's good news."

"I don't know if it's good news or bad news. I'm dreading that tournament. I couldn't care less about being a knight." He frowned at her. "Are you going to tell me why you're wearing my armor?" Mr. Cottonhorn's ears twitched. He seemed to be waiting for an explanation, too.

"Oh, right." She smiled again. Wouldn't Dexter be proud when he heard her story? "Well, this morning, I went to the blacksmith's to get the suit for you, as a surprise. But as you know, there are a lot of pieces, so I figured that wearing it was the easiest way to carry it."

"That was nice of you but…" He sneezed again. "Mom and Dad wouldn't approve. You could get into trouble."

"Don't worry. I wore the helmet the entire time, so no one knew it was me. In fact, they thought I was you." She glanced out the window. "I'd better change before Hunter gets back." She started to take off the pieces of plate armor, setting them on the floor next to Dexter's bed. Mr. Cottonhorn adjusted his glasses, picked up his book, and went back to reading.

"How come the suit's still covered in scratches and dings?" Dexter asked. "And that helmet doesn't look new."

As she slipped into the dress and adjusted her necklace, she told him about Betty's dad and the bunion.

"No new helmet for a few weeks?" Dexter sighed. "Well, it probably doesn't matter. I'm going to fail the jousting lesson anyway. I can't joust blind and I certainly can't joust if I have princely pox."

"Maybe you can," she said with a mischievous smile. Then, after sliding into her shoes, she sat on the edge of his bed.

"Huh?"

"Like I was saying, when I walked through the village, no one knew it was me. I kept the visor down the entire time. Even Dare thought he was talking to you."

Dexter scratched his forehead, looking a bit puzzled. "You talked to Dare while you were wearing my suit of armor? Didn't he recognize your voice?"

"Well, he did all the talking. You know how he is. And then he walked me straight to Hero Training."

"He did *what*?" Dexter managed to sit up this time, his eyes so wide they looked like they might burst through his glasses. For just a moment, he reminded her of Hopper Croakington II, son of the Frog Prince.

"That's the amazing news I wanted to tell you." She jumped to her feet. "Oh, Dex, it was so much fun! We got to choose horses, and we practiced riding up and down the field. Then we were given lances, and we practiced charging at a dummy and shield. The shield had a bull's-eye painted on it, and I hit it every time. I got a nearly perfect score. Professor Knight said I was the most improved student!" She squirmed with delight. "Can you believe it? I'm the most improved! I mean, *you're* the most improved, because they thought I was you."

While Mr. Cottonhorn turned a page, not a word or a sound came from Dexter. He sat perfectly still, his mouth wide open, as if a freezing curse had hit him. Was he breathing?

"Dex?"

Then, with a spray of spit, the words flew out. "You did *what?*" he cried. "How could you do that? Are you crazy?"

Darling frowned. "Of course I'm not crazy. Why are you so upset? This is good news. Professor Knight

gave you the highest score today." She didn't understand her brother's reaction. Surely he'd see that she'd helped him. Maybe the princely pox had infected his brain and he wasn't thinking clearly. "Are you... mad at me?" He'd never been mad at her before. Her eyes suddenly welled with tears.

Dexter took a deep breath. "Don't cry. Please don't cry. I'm not mad. I'm just confused." He repositioned his glasses and looked at his sister with wonder. "Did you say that you got a nearly perfect score?" She nodded. "You rode a horse while wearing a full suit of armor and you didn't fall off?" She nodded again. "And you carried a lance?"

"Yep."

"How is that possible? You've never done anything like that before."

She looked down at her feet.

"Wait a minute? Are you telling me that you're just like Dare? You don't have to practice? You do everything perfectly the first time? Am I the only

Charming who's not perfect?" He slumped against the pillows.

"No, no, that's not it. I'm nowhere near perfect. Believe me, I have to practice. I practice all the time." She sat back on the bed. "You know how Betty asked me about my calluses?" She held out her hands. "And you remember how I started climbing out of the tower when we were little?" He nodded. "Well, I'm still doing it."

"Here? At school?"

"Uh-huh. And there's more. I've been lifting weights and working out. And at night, I've been sneaking off campus and riding with Sir Gallopad." She stopped talking. His face was turning red. For a moment, she thought he was going to get angry because she'd kept so many secrets from him. They were the best of friends. Would he feel betrayed?

But instead he started laughing. Relieved, she laughed, too.

"I thought you'd left all that behind at Charming

Castle," he said. "Can you imagine what Mom and Dad would say?"

"I don't have to imagine. I know *exactly* what they'd say, which is why they'll never know what happened today."

After a few more sneezes, he looked at her, all joviality gone. "I guess I'd better get used to being number three."

Darling's heart suddenly ached. Had she hurt her brother's feelings? Dexter was no longer second best. Now he was third best. "I'm sorry. I didn't mean to…" But she *had* meant to succeed. When she'd sat on Sir Gallopad and held the lance, she'd wanted to be the best. She'd wanted to prove that she was equally able. But the painful, defeated look in her brother's eyes had turned success bittersweet. "As soon as you get your new helmet, you'll joust better than me. You'll see."

"What if I can't?" He swept his hair from his forehead. "It's bad enough that I fell off the horse in front of everyone, but now, thanks to you, they'll

expect me to be better than I am." He sighed. "At least we don't have class again until Thursday." Then he closed his eyes and yawned. "I'm so sleepy."

She'd messed things up. Not only had she taken a great risk by wearing the armor, but in her desire to help, she'd also put more pressure on Dexter by raising everyone's expectations. That was the last thing she'd intended. "I'm sorry," she told him. "I guess I messed things up." But he didn't hear her apology, because he'd started to snore. Mr. Cottonhorn was fast asleep, too.

She looked at her brother's splotchy face. "I promise I'll make things right," she whispered. *But how?*

A Cry

for Help

Darling slipped into the Damsel-In-Distressing classroom and claimed a vacant spot at the end of a velvet settee. Back in her dorm room, she'd had just enough time to shower off the sweat and grime from jousting. Then she'd dressed in a powder-blue frock with a ruffled hem, a silver belt, silver boots, and her sapphire tiara. No one questioned her change of clothing since breakfast. It was a princess's right to change outfits as many times a day as she wanted.

Apple passed around a platter of mini apple tarts. Having missed lunch, Darling grabbed a handful and tried not to eat too quickly. Because she was once again in princess mode, ravenous consumption was frowned upon. Delicate nibbling was expected. But when no one was looking, she shoved an entire tart into her mouth. Then another.

"Did you hear about Dexter?" Ashlynn asked the girls.

Darling stopped chewing. "My brother?"

"Yes, your brother. Hunter told me that Dexter was amazing in Hero Training today. Maybe even better than Daring."

Apple set the platter aside. "That's silly. Daring's destiny is to be the most charming prince ever after."

Ashlynn poured herself some sparkling cloud water. "What did he do that was so amazing?"

"I heard about it, too," Cerise said under the hood of her red cape. "They were learning how to joust, and Dexter was the best in class."

"But he's so not athletic," Briar said as she stretched out on one of the couches. "Who could have guessed that a hero was hiding behind those glasses?"

"He does have dreamy eyes," Holly said. She smiled at Darling. "Your brothers are sooooo cute."

Darling ate another tart, not offering an opinion about the handsomeness of her brothers. Duchess Swan didn't add to the conversation, either. She sat separately from the others and wore her usual sneer.

"Good afternoon, girls." Madam Maid Marian sauntered into the room. She wore her signature cone hat and veil. But, like last time, it was oddly paired with her tunic and leggings. It seemed as if she couldn't quite decide whether she should dress the damsel or dress the rebel. She tossed her black bag aside, then helped herself to a tart. As she sat on her desk, her legs swung freely. "So who can tell me what the lesson is for today?"

Holly pressed a button on her MirrorPad. "It says in our syllabus that we're supposed to work on crying for help." Then she read the instructions out loud:

Class: Damsel-In-Distressing

Lesson: A Cry for Help

Obstacles, such as a thick briar patch or pea-soup fog, can make it difficult for the rescuer to locate the damsel. Thus a good strong set of vocal cords is handy indeed. Calling "Help!" at the top of her lungs will guide the rescuer in the right direction.

Instructions: Take turns standing in front of the classroom and crying for help. The loudest gets hextra credit. Try to avoid laryngitis, for a damsel who is unable to scream may miss out on her rescue and not get her Happily Ever After.

Apple volunteered to go first. She stood in front of the class, smoothed her hair, then said, *"Help, help."*

Madam Maid Marian shook her head. "You sound like you're in a library. Surely you can turn up the volume."

"But I've always been taught to use my *inside* voice," Apple said sweetly.

Darling had been taught the same lesson. A *Charming princess should be seen, not heard.*

"Well, this is the exception to that stupid—" Madam Maid Marian cleared her throat. "I mean, this is the exception to that traditional rule." She strode onto the stage. "The trick is to take the deepest breath you can manage, then force the sound by using your diaphragm." She cupped her hands around her mouth and hollered, "*Help!*"

Apple frowned. "But why should I yell? I'm going to be in a glass coffin, practically in a coma, after eating a poisoned apple. So yelling makes no sense."

"And I'm going to be inside a big, bad wolf," Cerise said with a slight growl. "I don't think it's possible to yell and be heard from in there, is it?"

Madam Maid Marian threw her hands in the air. "Oh, come on, ladies. This is a chance to let your hair down."

"Let my hair down? I'll do it!" Holly hurried to the front of the room. "*Help! Help!*" she yelled.

Duchess elbowed her way between them. "I don't even have a rescuer, but this looks like fun. *Heeeeeelp!* And I'm a dancer, so of course I have amazing lung capacity. *Heeeeeelp!*"

Briar climbed up onto the desk and started hollering. Ashlynn stood on a couch and joined in the cacophony. Even Apple found her *outside* voice. But Darling sat quietly. The scene made her very uncomfortable. She was used to acting un-princesslike, but never in public.

"Come on," Madam Maid Marian said, waving for her to join the others.

"What in Ever After is going on in here?" Headmaster Grimm strode into the room. The girls fell silent. "I'm getting complaints from the other teachers that a great disturbance is coming from this very classroom. Damsels should not be disruptive. What are you teaching them, Professor Marian?"

"I'm following the recommended curriculum," she said. "We are practicing calling for help."

"I see." He nodded. "Then that is most appropriate. Carry on." Once again, the room was filled with shouting, hollering, and screaming. Darling, however, remained on the settee. She could yell as well as the rest of them. But after being a hero for the morning, screaming for help felt so…humiliating.

Madam Maid Marian didn't press her to join the others. But when class was dismissed, she said, "See you all on Thursday for our final lesson before Parents Weekend. Ms. Charming, I would like to speak with you."

Once they were alone, Darling hung her head. "I'm sorry I didn't participate. I don't think my parents would approve of my making so much noise."

"Perhaps not. But would they approve of your *other* activities?" Darling tried to hide her surprise. Madam Maid Marian raised an eyebrow. "You don't have to act the part for me. I know a Rebel when I see one."

"Rebel?" Darling squared her shoulders. "I'm not a *Rebel*."

Madam Maid Marian opened her black bag and pulled out an arrow. The shaft was made from pale birch, and three green feathers were bound to the end. It was exactly like the arrow Darling had found at her feet that very morning in the Enchanted Forest.

Had Madam Maid Marian seen Darling riding?

They each paused, as if to measure the other's reaction. "I understand that your brother has princely pox," Madam Maid Marian said, breaking the silence. "And yet he was able to ride a horse and hit a target dead on. Who knew that Dexter could be capable of such a show of strength?"

"He's a much better athlete than everyone thinks," Darling said.

"And perhaps you're not as quiet as everyone thinks." She pushed her veil aside and winked. "Guess you truly can't judge a book by its cover."

Darling gulped. "I guess not."

Banned

Books

At an early age, Darling had become an expert at judging a book by its cover. Well, one book, to be specific. If the cover was made of pink leather, the title embossed in gold leaf, and the whole thing covered in glitter, then she knew, without reading a single page, that the book belonged to a particular set known as the Princess Collection. And that it would bore her to tears.

The Princess Collection, Volumes 1 to 10, contained all the famous traditional princess stories—

the ones full of rescues and Happily Ever Afters. The Charming Committee on Appropriate Reading Material had given this collection its gold-star approval rating. And so, each night before she went to bed, Darling was read a story from one of the volumes. But when she learned to read on her own, she ignored the Princess Collection and grabbed one of Dexter's graphic novels instead. The librarian was hastily summoned.

"My daughter is in need of proper reading material," Queen Charming explained.

The librarian was a woman named Madam Grimm, descended from the famous bookish Grimms. Madam Grimm was the executive librarian at the village library, where she kept order with her magical *shhh*. Anyone on the receiving end of one of her shushes would not be able to utter a word until leaving the library.

The queen, Darling, and Dexter had walked to the castle's foyer to greet the librarian. As round as she was tall, Madam Grimm wore a stretchy pantsuit and casual loafers. Her eyeglasses were as large as saucers. "Hello, children," she said with a bright smile.

"Hello," they replied. Dexter was so excited about getting some new books that his glasses fogged up. Darling yawned. She already knew what the librarian would bring her—some old, boring story that she'd already read.

"En garde!" Daring and King Charming charged into the foyer, their swords raised. Daring jumped onto a table and knocked over a vase of flowers. The king advanced with a circular parry, slicing through a candelabra in the process. Madam Grimm ducked as Daring's counterparry nearly sliced an inch off her beehive hairdo.

"My dear," the queen said to her husband, "must you do that here? We have a guest." She pointed to the librarian, who was looking rather alarmed by the sudden increase in violent activity.

The king glanced at the librarian's cart, which was full of books. Then he pointed his blade at Dexter.

"You're not going to waste time reading, are you? Haven't you got mountains to climb? Horses to train? Dragons to slay?"

"But, Dad," Dexter said, "I like reading."

"Sire," Madam Grimm said with a scowl. She patted her hair back into place. "Reading is *never* a waste of time. In fact, I think it would be advisable if your elder son took up the activity every once in a while."

"If I'm going to read something, I think it should be a book about me," Daring said. "Has anyone written my biography yet?" Then he slashed the air with his sword, knocking the head off a nearby statue. When the head hit the stone floor, the royal hounds began barking.

"There is too much commotion in here," the queen said apologetically. "Please, come into the sitting room." She ushered Madam Grimm down the hall and into a plush room with a breathtaking view of the eastern mountain chain. "I'm eager to see what you've brought the children."

"Did you bring me the latest Super Prince?" Dexter asked, practically bouncing off the walls. Darling settled on the couch. Dexter would lend her his copy when he'd finished. In secret, of course.

Madam Grimm plucked a book from the cart and held it up to the chandelier's light. "For the young prince, who loves adventure stories, I've brought an illustrated edition of *Escape from Minotaur Mine*."

Dexter grabbed it. "Wow, thanks!"

"You also get a pop-up edition of *Dragons Near and Far*, a new mystery called *Mayhem on the Fairy-tale Express*, and...the latest book in the Super Prince series."

Dexter cheered. He collected all the books, ran to the corner, and began reading.

Darling's fingers felt twitchy. She wanted to grab one of her brother's books. She loved hero stories. *And* adventure stories. *And* mysteries. And if she had to read one more helpless-damsel-gets-rescued-by-true-love-and-lives-happily-ever-after story, she'd scream!

"What have you brought for my daughter?" Queen Charming asked.

"Something truly fitting such a perfect princess." The librarian held up a book with a glittery pink cover and gold-embossed title. A groan emerged from Darling, the likes of which had never been heard at Charming Castle.

"My darling," the queen said worriedly. "Are you ill?"

The groan reached a crescendo, then Darling took a huge breath of air. "*Cinderella?*" she shrieked, pointing at the pink book. "Are you kidding me? I've read it a zillion times. Shall I sum it up for you? Unhappy girl meets prince, gets rescued by prince, then they live happily forever after. There's nothing new. It's boring! It's the most boring story in the entire world!" Dexter looked up from his book, as surprised as everyone else in the room. Darling was throwing a royal fit. "I want to read a book about a princess who goes on a quest. Who has an adventure for once in her life."

"Those stories do not exist," the queen said. "Now, sit down and stop hollering. Princesses do not holler."

"Actually…" The librarian adjusted her enormous glasses. "Those stories *do* exist."

"Really?" Darling couldn't believe it.

"Yes, indeed. There are many stories about the Amazonian Queen and how she ruled her nation of female warriors. And there is the story of Artemis, a young goddess who could hunt with a bow and arrow. My favorite would be the story of Atalanta, who could run faster than almost any man. And Maid Marian recently wrote about her adventures in the Sherwood Forest."

"I want to read those stories," Darling said. "All of them. Right now. May I? Please?"

Madam Grimm shook her head. "They are banned, I'm afraid, in your kingdom. The Charming Committee does not approve of such literature."

"But—"

"That's enough of that," the queen said, rising to

her feet. "Thank you for bringing such lovely, appropriate books. I shall have the butler escort you to the front door." She rang a small bell.

Madam Grimm set the pink *Cinderella* book on the couch next to Darling. "Happy reading." Then, pushing her wheeled cart, she followed the butler out of the sitting room.

Darling looked pleadingly at her mother. But the queen was not swayed. "Your big blue eyes will not change the fact that we have traditions to uphold, my darling," the queen said. "Your temper tantrum was not befitting a Charming princess. I am most displeased." Then, with a swift turn on her heel, she glided from the room, her gown rustling as if it were also displeased.

That night, as Darling got ready for bed, a gentle knock sounded on her door. When she opened it, she found, not a person, but a book lying on the floor. It wasn't a pink book. It was called *Secrets of the Sherwood Forest* by Maid Marian. The cover showed a woman dressed in pants and boots, holding a bow and arrow. Darling grabbed the book, then quickly closed the door.

She hugged the book to her chest and smiled. "Thank you, Dexter," she whispered. He'd come to her rescue, just as he'd promised.

Chapter 15

Squire Darling to the Rescue

Thursday followed Wednesday, as it tended to do, except for that one time when the Science and Sorcery class accidentally conjured a time spell and the days of the week got jumbled. Thursday meant that there'd be a meeting of both Hero Training and Damsel-In-Distressing. Darling didn't have to worry about the hero class, because firstly, she wasn't a hero, and secondly, she'd had no right impersonating her brother and attending class in his name. Seriously,

that had been wrong. And she should never do any-thing like that again.

She called Dexter. Hunter answered his Mirror-Phone and said that Dexter was still sick in bed. As she showered and dressed, one question spun around in her mind. How could she make things right for her brother? When he did go back to class, he'd be expected to joust with nearly perfect precision. Maybe he could learn to match her skills eventually, but not by this weekend! What could be done to save him from further embarrassment?

Only one answer came to her, and though she debated it over and over, it seemed to be the only solution. It would require more risk, but that didn't worry Darling. These days, *Risk* was practically her middle name.

She couldn't wait to share her plan with Dexter. After a hurried breakfast of lumpy porridge, she headed to her brother's dorm room. Along the way she accepted two boxes of chocolates, caused a fight to break out, and was handed a rather prickly up-rooted rosebush. "Uh, thanks," she said.

Up ahead, a group of boys crossed the commons, with Daring in the lead. Dressed in their suits of armor, helmets tucked under their arms, they were stirring up quite a bit of attention. Even Darling stopped to watch the procession. No matter which side of the aisle you stood, Royal or Rebel, the knight in shining armor was one of the most cele-brated characters in the fairytale world. As the morning sun glinted off their chain mail and crests, a little shiver darted up her spine.

Today it was her turn to be the hero, for she was determined to save Dexter's reputation.

Well, actually, she was determined to *ruin* it.

Darling's idea was this. Because of her nearly flaw-less display in class, she'd set a standard that Dexter could never meet. Even if he had a new visor that fit over his glasses, the truth was that Dexter possessed a very different skill set than his brother or sister did. It was stressful enough that everyone expected him to be number two, but now they expected him to be better than he could ever be.

So Darling's answer was to go to Hero Training class dressed as Dexter and erase her previous performance. She'd miss the target, she'd lose her balance, and she'd show everyone that it had been a fluke and that Dexter was back to his old self. Then, when he got over princely pox and returned to class, everyone's expectations would be back to normal.

She knocked on the door, and when no one answered, she tiptoed in. "Dex?" she whispered. Hunter was with the other Hero Training students, and Mr. Cottonhorn was nowhere to be seen. Dexter, however, was in bed, fast asleep. The spots on his face had gone from a pale blue to royal blue, which was more fitting his complexion, but still looked weird. His medicine sat on the bedside table. She glanced at the red warning label: CAUSES DROWSINESS.

Poor guy. Should she wake him? Her hand floated above his shoulder. What if she woke him and he

told her not to go to Hero Training? What if he forbade her? She tapped a finger on her chin. Perhaps she shouldn't wake him. After all, sleep was important. It would be selfish of her to interrupt his recovery. She'd go to class, then come back and tell him the good news—that once again, Professor Knight and the students didn't expect more from him than second-best.

And so, after slipping into her workout shirt and pants, and tucking her dress, heels, and tiara under Dexter's bed, she put on the armor. Then she flipped her hair, slowing time so she could run down the hall and get to the field just as class was beginning.

"Dexter?" Hunter said as Darling strode toward him. "What are you doing here? You looked terrible this morning. I thought you were too sick to joust."

She didn't have to respond, because her brother stepped in. "Charmings are *never* too sick," Daring said as he checked his reflection in her visor. "We have superior immune systems. How does my hair look? Do I have helmet hair?"

"Squires!" Professor Knight rode onto the field. His horse was a swaybacked old thing with a white beard that matched his own. "Gather ye round." The students clustered together, their faces turned up toward the professor. Darling was the only student wearing a helmet. "On this day, which is today, thou shalt face one another on the field." Then he looked directly at Darling. "Squire Charming, how good of you to join us. A true knight would never allow a little malady like princely pox to slow him down. Be it known that I once jousted when I had an inflamed hangnail." Then Professor Knight explained the jousting rules.

The field was divided by a short fence, which prevented the horses from colliding. Two riders competed at a time. They took their places on opposite ends of the fence, facing each other. A shield was held in one hand, a lance in the other. The horses had been trained to ride the length of the fence, so there was no need for reins. When the trumpet blasted, each rider hollered: "Charge!" The goal was to hit the opponent's shield with the lance. Hitting the shield and breaking your own lance earned the highest score. Hitting the shield and unhorsing the opponent earned the second-highest score. But missing the shield earned a big, fat fairy-fail.

"Be advised," Professor Knight said, "that whilst your lances are sharp, Professor Rumpelstiltskin hath placed a safety spell on each one. Thus there wilt be no skewering of flesh in this class." An audible sigh of relief rose among the students. "Squire Charming and I shall now demonstrate."

Daring and the professor took their places. Daring's steed was young and muscular. The professor's horse was bowlegged and arthritic. This didn't seem like a fair match. But when the trumpet sounded, the old horse managed to summon a surprising show of strength. "Charge!" Dust rose from beneath their hooves as they thundered along the fence. Daring's aim was perfect, hitting the professor's shield in the exact center. But the professor's aim was equally exact. Each lance cracked in two, the tips flying through the air. Daring whipped off his helmet. With a shake of his head, his locks fell perfectly into place. Then both he and the professor bowed. Everyone cheered.

And so it went that each student took his turn riding the course. Quite a few missed the shield entirely. A few others were unhorsed by direct shield hits. Darling couldn't risk being unhorsed, for that could mean possible injury, which would lead to her identity being discovered. How could she lower the professor's expectations but avoid being hit at the same time?

It would soon be her turn. She looked around for Sir Gallopad. Where was he? "Take my horse," Daring said, offering his steed.

She shook her head. There was no time to learn the nuances of a different horse. She and Sir Gallopad were perfectly suited. And he'd get jealous if she chose another. But where was he? An odd movement on the horizon caught her eye. She peered through her visor, then smiled. Sir Gallopad was using his camouflage skills so he could graze in peace. His legs blended into the tall grass, while his upper body blended into the distant forest. She whistled. As he raised his head, his body turned jet-black. Then he joined her on the field.

Hunter slapped her back. "Good luck, roomie." He mounted his horse. "I'll try not to maim you." It was all in good fun, but truthfully, thanks to all the ax-throwing, Hunter was one powerful guy. Darling decided to add firewood chopping to her workout routine.

"Looks like you found yourself a good horse," Daring said. She nodded. He set a footstool next to Sir Gallopad. "Good luck."

As she stepped onto the footstool, she remembered to act like Dexter. So she pretended to be a bit wobbly. Only after the third try, and a big groan, did she manage to pull herself onto the saddle. Daring handed up the shield, then the lance. "You're not too sick? You gonna be okay?" She nodded. "That's the spirit!"

Hunter waited on the other end of the field. She went over the plan in her head. To lower expectations, she would hit Hunter's shield, but not hard enough to break the lance. At the same time, she would send most of her strength to her legs, so as not to fall from the saddle. She took a deep breath. The trumpet was raised. Her adrenaline soared. She tightened her grip on the lance. This would be her last chance—her only chance to joust. Never again would she have this opportunity. Today she was a knight. Tomorrow and for the rest of her life she'd be a damsel.

And as the trumpet blasted, Darling's plan was shattered.

A Charming Confession

"I don't believe it." Dexter spit a thermometer from his mouth. "Is this a joke? Tell me it's a joke."

Darling yanked off the helmet and tossed it aside. "I'll explain everything, but first I've got to change before Hunter comes back." Dexter was sitting up in bed. A Castleteria tray, two empty bottles of Jack Frost Glacier Water, and a dozen comic books lay on the floor. Darling made a mental note to ask Apple about those cleaning dwarves. Mr. Cottonhorn, the jackalope, was sitting on the windowsill, munching

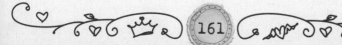

on a bundle of carrot tops. "By the way, you jousted against Hunter today and you won."

Dexter gasped. "I did *what?*"

"It was a bull's-eye hit. Center of the shield. The lance split perfectly." She pulled the chain-mail tunic over her head. "You were amazing. Everyone congratulated you. You got the highest score! Again! Think how impressed Raven will be when she hears."

Dexter folded his arms. He didn't say anything. She reached under his bed and grabbed her dress, shoes, and tiara. Then she quickly changed in the bathroom. "I know you told me not to go," she said as she borrowed a comb and tried to refluff her hair. "But I had to, Dex. I wanted to help you and—"

"This isn't about me," he grumbled.

"Of course it's about you. I messed things up, so I was trying to make them right. I—" She stared into the bathroom mirror, gazing into her own blue eyes. "I—" During the joust, she hadn't been thinking about Dexter. But she *had* been thinking about how much fun she was having. How thrilling it felt. She'd forgotten her plan. She dropped the comb into the sink. "You're right." She stepped back into the room. "This was about me. I'm so sorry. Now I've royally messed things up."

A clanging sound echoed in the hallway. The dorm room door flew open, and Hunter walked in, still dressed in his armor. He looked confused when he spied Dexter lying in bed, but he didn't ask any questions. Instead, he pointed toward the hall. "King Charming is on the way."

"Dad?" both Darling and Dexter said. But there was no time to get their stories straight and no time for Darling to flip her hair and escape, because King Charming was already standing in the doorway. He was dressed in a pin-striped suit and a black dress shirt. He wore his crown, of course. A Charming never leaves the castle without a crown. Darling quickly grabbed her tiara and plopped it back on her head.

"Hello, children," the king said. Dexter scrambled out of bed and shook his hand.

"It's very nice to see you," Darling said with a curtsy. "But what are you doing here? Parents Weekend doesn't start until tomorrow."

"I came early to meet with the headmaster. He needs additional funding, and we Charmings always seem to have the deepest pockets." He pointed to the windowsill. "Does that bunny have horns?"

"Yes," Dexter said.

"How odd." He walked over to the window and looked outside. "I see that the Evil Queen's daughter is walking in the garden. Her family must be very disappointed with her rebellious ways. Flipping the script is not something a Charming would do."

Darling squeezed Dexter's arm to let him know that his secret crush was safe with her.

King Charming glanced at his Royalex watch. "I have a few minutes before my next meeting, so I thought I'd check on Dexter." He frowned at his son. "Your mother has been worried. We heard you had princely pox. I assume you are bravely fighting

the illness and are on the verge of victory." He slapped Dexter on the back.

Dexter coughed. "Uh, yes, sir." His hand flew to his nose as he held back a sneeze.

"Excellent and expected news." The king turned his attention to Hunter. "I see you've just come from Hero Training class. Are you learning to joust?"

"Yes, sire," Hunter said.

"You are destined to be a woodsman by trade, so the knightly skills are not expected of you. However, you father was surprisingly adept on horseback. And a Huntsman is destined to be a hero, even if he is not a knight. Are you following in his footsteps?"

"I'm doing my best…er, sire." Hunter stumbled on his words. He occasionally forgot how royalty like to be addressed—must be all that time he spent in the woods. But your son is definitely following in *your* footsteps. He was the best in class today. A perfect score."

"That is no surprise. Daring was last year's champion. He will, of course, be the best this year, too."

"Actually, sire, I meant your *other* son."

Everyone turned and looked at Dexter. Standing there in his pajamas, his nose red from sneezing and with a terrible case of bedhead, he didn't look anything like a jousting champion. The blue spots weren't helping, either.

Darling stared worriedly at Dexter. What would he say? Would he tell the truth? Truth would be a catastrophe. She'd get in trouble for dressing in his armor. He'd get in trouble for allowing it to happen. Shame, disappointment, and disapproval would pelt them like hail. She chewed her lower lip, unsure what to do.

But before Dexter could say anything, Hunter stepped forward. "It was amazing, sire. Even though Dexter's been sick, he went to class. He jousted against me and won. Professor Knight said it was the best he'd ever seen."

"Really?" Darling said, bursting into a proud smile. "He said *the best*?"

"Yeah. But Dexter ran off the field before Professor Knight could commend him. He said that Dexter had the potential to win the tournament."

King Charming did not congratulate his second-born son. Rather, he narrowed his eyes, a stern expression tightening his handsome face. Dexter just stood there, looking completely lost, as if he'd woken from a sleeping curse and had no idea what was going on or where he was.

"How come you ran off the field?" Hunter asked.

"Uh…" Dexter scratched one of the blue spots.

Darling cleared her throat. "He was feeling sick. Isn't that right, Dex? You needed to come back and get some rest. That's why you're in your pajamas." She took his arm and guided him back into bed. "I agree that you need more rest." Then she whispered in his ear, "Don't worry. It's going to be okay."

"Win the tournament?" he whispered between clenched teeth. "How am I supposed to do that?"

Darling pulled the blanket up to his chin and said

loudly, "That's right, you need to sleep now. Nighty-night." Then she turned to her father. "Who wants to go to the Castleteria and get a bite to eat? If you drown Hagatha's beetloaf in ketchup, it's almost edible."

"My darling daughter, I need to speak to your brother in private. Please wait outside. You, too, Mr. Huntsman."

With heavy steps, Darling left the room. Hunter shut the door behind them. "This armor is hot," Hunter complained as he removed his chain mail tunic. Then, bare-chested, he leaned against the wall. Like Daring, Hunter enjoyed showing off his best assets. But he wasn't trying to woo her. "Your dad didn't look happy that Dexter did so well. What's the deal?"

"Shhh," Darling told him as she pressed her ear to the door. "I'm trying to hear."

Despite the thick panel of wood that stood between them, King Charming's voice rang clear from inside the dorm room. "Your mother and I have been worried about you, son. All those years of reading comic books and playing MirrorGames, we were beginning to think you weren't cut from the same cloth as the other Charming men. I'm very proud to hear of your accomplishments today. Tomorrow, two Charmings will joust for the championship."

Darling gasped. She turned to Hunter. "What did my father mean when he said that *two* Charmings will joust tomorrow?"

"Since Dexter was the best in class, he has to joust the champion."

The champion was Daring. Oh my fairy godmother, what had she done? She pressed her ear to the door again. Dexter was talking. "Dad, I'm feeling sick. This princely pox is super itchy. I don't think I can joust tomorrow."

"Nonsense! A Charming is never too sick. It is destiny that my sons should be the best. I've never felt prouder."

Darling's heart sank. *I'm the one you should be proud of*, she thought.

"However," King Charming said, "it is your brother's destiny to be the champion. You are destined to be second best. If you are as good as Professor Knight claims, and he is usually correct in his observations, then tomorrow you must throw the match."

"Throw the match?" Darling said with surprise. Had she said that aloud? *Oops.*

The door suddenly opened. Darling stumbled backward, bumping into Hunter. Her father stepped into the hallway. He scowled at her. "Eavesdropping is not princess-like," he said.

"Sorry," she told him with another curtsy.

"And whatever is the matter with your hair? It looks as if you've been wearing a bowl over your head. And why is your dress all rumpled? Didn't we pay extra for ironing fairies? Make certain that you look appropriate for your brothers' tournament tomorrow." Then he looked at Hunter. "Mr. Huntsman?"

Hunter stepped forward. "Yes, uh, sire?"

"Tomorrow you will make sure that Dexter is out of bed and dressed on time. Two Charmings on the

field! It will be quite a glorious day for the Charming family."

As the king strode down the hall and out of the dormitory, Darling dashed back into her brother's room. "Throw the match? That's so unfair."

"What do you mean, it's unfair?" Dexter lay on the bed, staring up at the ceiling. "This whole thing is unfair."

"But I could win," she said with a stomp of her foot. "I know I could. Why should I have to throw the match?"

"You're not throwing the match," Dexter said. "Because there is absolutely, positively, one hundred percent no way I'm letting you wear my armor ever again."

"But—?" She turned. Hunter was standing right next to her. He looked shocked.

"What do you mean you won't let her wear your armor *again*?" he said.

*E*vening glided in as gracefully as a princess. The swans at the Swan Lake tucked their beaks into their wings and closed their black eyes. Tree frogs all over campus joined in a twilight chorus, and students settled into their dorm rooms.

Darling sat at her desk, staring at a hextbook page. She had no idea what she'd just read. Why couldn't she focus? Rosabella was hunched over her own desk, studying a thick stack of legal documents. "Did you know that the only kingdom that gives

citizenship to beasts is Wonderland?" She pounded her fist on the desk. "That is so unfair. I'm going to get my law degree and fix that."

"Uh-huh" was as much enthusiasm as Darling could muster. Certainly beasts had problems to deal with, but at the moment, she was preoccupied with her own troubles.

Hunter was suspicious for good reason—he'd overheard some of her and Dexter's conversation. When he asked, "What do you mean you won't let her wear your armor *again?*" Darling did the only thing she could—she pretended to faint.

Fainting had been mastered in the last quarter's Damsel-In-Distressing class. Not the real kind, where you actually lose consciousness, but the fake kind that comes in handy in many damsel situations. Before she hit the floor, Hunter swooped in and caught her while Dexter ran and got her a glass of cold water and a damp washcloth for her forehead. Hero Training had paid off. Then Hunter escorted her to Damsel-In-Distressing class. "Look, Darling, I know something odd is going on. How could Dexter beat me in jousting when he's so sick that he can barely sit up in bed?" She looked the other way. "And how come he told you that he forbade you to wear his armor...*again?*" She pretended to get a hext on her MirrorPhone. "Wait a spell." He stopped walking. "If Dexter was sick in bed, and you were wearing his armor, then..." His eyes widened. "Did you...?"

She put her hands on her hips. "Are you asking if I pretended to be Dexter? That would mean that I jousted against you and won." She forced herself to laugh. "Oh, that's so silly, Hunter. That's the silliest thing I've ever heard."

His expression relaxed. Then he laughed. "Yeah. Ridiculous. I must have hit my head during practice." He walked her to the classroom door and left.

In Damsel-In-Distressing, Madam Maid Marian had them watch a movie called *Pride and Properness*. But Darling was distracted with worry. What if Hunter kept asking questions and Dexter, in his

daze of sickness, accidentally confessed that Darling had been the knight in dented armor? Hunter would tell Ashlynn, who'd tell the other princesses, and Darling would end up in the headmaster's office, facing her parents, who would be upset that she'd put herself in danger. They'd also be royally miffed that she'd broken countless rules, and that she'd damaged the family's reputation. She'd end up back in the Charming Castle tower for sure!

And then there was Dexter's dilemma. Suffering from princely pox was a perfectly reasonable excuse to get out of a jousting tournament. But now, thanks to her meddling, he couldn't use that excuse, because everyone believed he was some sort of Super Prince and had no problem jousting while sick. There was no getting out of tomorrow's tournament, unless his arms fell off, but that was not a side effect of his medication, so there was no counting on that!

So much fretting made the Damsel-In-Distressing class drag on and on. Darling only realized it was

over when Briar elbowed her. "Hey, it's time to go."

Back in her dorm room, the evening was also dragging. Rosabella seemed engrossed in her studies. But for Darling, the words on the page could not hold her interest, and the room began to feel small. Her legs twitched. She wanted to run. But there was no way she'd risk sneaking off campus, not with her father staying in the Parents' Quarters.

She pushed her chair away from her desk. "I'm hungry," she said. "Do you want anything?"

"How about a pack of beanstalk crisps?" Rosabella said. "But only if they're organic. And only if they've been harvested from a fair-trade field."

Darling tied her bathrobe sash, slipped her feet into a pair of fuzzy slippers, then went down the hall. The Royal Common Room was empty. The fire had burned down to embers and was the only source of light. She walked behind the oak tree that grew in the corner. "Oh, hi," she said as a figure stepped out of the darkness. "You startled me."

Raven Queen smiled. "Sorry. I often have that

effect on people." She held out a bottle of lemonade. "I was thirsty." Then she took a long swig. No wonder Darling hadn't seen her. Raven's hair, bathrobe, and slippers were as dark as the shadows that filled the room. "What are you going to get?" She tilted her head toward the vending machine.

"Beanstalk crisps," Darling said as she pushed a button. A bag dropped into the bin.

"Oh, sea salt and vinegar. Those are good. I think I'll get some, too. General Villainy thronework always gives me the munchies. Evil spelling burns a lot of calories, even though I would rather be burning them another way." She grabbed a bag. "How are things going with Dexter?"

"Dexter?" What had Raven meant by that question? Did she know something? Had she been talking to Hunter? "What sorts of *things* are you asking about?"

"I heard he was sick."

"Oh, of course." She sighed with relief. "He has princely pox."

"Ugh, that's rough." She took another drink. "Apple was saying that Dexter's been really good at jousting. I was kind of surprised. I mean, I never thought of him as a knight."

Was Raven impressed? It was hard to tell since she wore a serious look most of the time. Could jousting be a way for Dexter to win her heart? "Yeah, I guess he's a natural," Darling lied. "Do you like knights?"

"They really don't matter much to me. I didn't read those stories when I was little. Why would I? No knight is written into my story."

"Oh," Darling said. Knighthood wasn't going to win Raven's heart after all. "Consider yourself lucky. Not having a knight in your story means that you don't have to wait to be rescued."

"I would never wait. That's not my style." Then she smiled, and her dark eyes twinkled. "The kind of guy I want, when I'm ready for one, is an equal partner. Someone who can think for himself and is okay with my thinking for myself. Someone who's clever and kind. Someone who—I hope you don't think

I'm being rude—but someone who is the opposite of your brother Daring. All that fighting and boasting and stomping around isn't what I'm looking for. But there seem to be a lot of girls around here who are."

The boy Raven had just described was Dexter!

Darling hadn't spent much one-on-one time with the Evil Queen's daughter. If King Charming caught them talking, Darling would get an earful about hanging out with the wrong sort. Her parents would worry that Raven's rebellious attitude would rub off on their daughter. *Wouldn't they be shocked to learn that I've been equally rebellious?* Darling thought.

"Well, I'd better get back to studying," Raven said. Darling grabbed a second bag of crisps, and the girls walked up the hall together. "Tell Dexter I hope he feels better soon."

"Okay." He'd be over the moon to hear that Raven had asked about him. "I will."

Back in her room, she handed a bag of crisps to Rosabella, then settled on her bed to eat the other bag. The conversation with Raven had been a nice distraction and had glimmered with the possibility of future friendship, but her thoughts darted back to tomorrow's tournament. She couldn't help but feel that she was about to miss out on the opportunity of a lifetime.

Dexter was a Prince Charming, but he clearly wasn't cut out to be a knight. Even if he had a new visor that fit over his glasses, he didn't have the desire to be a knight, and desire was just as important as skill. But she did. She'd loved the feel of the armor. She'd loved gripping the shield and lance, galloping across that field. And she was good—the best Professor Knight had ever seen.

Her MirrorPhone buzzed. It was a hext from Madam Maid Marian.

Meet me by the drawbridge in five minutes. Come alone. And wear your running shoes.

Darling narrowed her eyes. What was going on?

Marian by Moonlight

$\mathcal{M}$adam Maid Marian was waiting, her black bag in hand. "Are you ready?" she asked.

"Ready for what?"

"For an adventure in the Enchanted Forest."

Adventure? Darling looked around nervously. "I'm not supposed to have any *adventures*. They're too dangerous for a Charming princess."

"I see." Madam Maid Marian stepped close and looked right into Darling's eyes. "Are you telling me that you would rather go back to your dormitory room and practice *waiting*?"

"No. I..." Darling pulled her cloak tighter. She'd dressed her part, just in case she bumped into someone. Her gown and shoes were appropriately fancy, and her tiara was pinned in place. "I don't think I should leave campus. Not tonight. My dad's here, and if he finds out that I broke curfew, he'll flip his crown."

"But you're not breaking curfew if you're with me," Madam Maid Marian said with a grand sweep of her arm. "I'm a teacher and I'm giving you special permission. Also, I possess the secret password, so we'll have no trouble getting through the headmaster's security system."

"Headmaster Grimm gave you the password?" That seemed odd, since he clearly didn't approve of her.

"Gave?" She laughed. "Perhaps you aren't familiar with my past." Darling was quite familiar. She'd read and reread every chapter in Madam Maid Marian's

book. She almost forgot her teacher was one of Robin Hood's famous Merry Men, equally famous for *taking* as for giving.

Darling needed no further convincing. For the first time in her life, she was on the receiving end of an invitation to adventure. She burst into a smile. "Let's do it! Should we go to the stables for horses?"

"No, I'm much more comfortable in the forest on foot." After crossing the drawbridge, they reached the wall of briars. Madam Maid Marian stepped up to a particularly thorny briar and whispered to it. The plant shuddered, and then a tunnel magically appeared in the patch, wide enough for them to walk straight through. As soon as they'd reached the other side, the tunnel disappeared. Madam Maid Marian yanked her cone hat off her head. "Phew! I hate wearing that thing."

"Really?" Darling asked with surprise. They hurried down the path and toward the forest. "Then why do you wear it?"

"Same reason you're wearing that velvet gown. Appearances. If I want to keep my job at Ever After

High, I need to look the part. But I don't have to look the part while I'm in the woods. Nor do you. Are you wearing your silver suit?"

Darling stumbled. Then she tried to feign confusion. "Silver what?"

"Oh, come on, Ms. Charming. I saw you the other night, galloping like a jockey. I know all about the silver suit, which is lovely, by the way. Don't worry. I'm not a spy for the headmaster. In case you hadn't noticed, he and I don't see eye to eye on some things."

Darling stopped walking. Just like with Betty Bunyan back at the blacksmith's shop, Darling felt as if she'd met a kindred soul. Here was a woman who could appreciate the soft, stretchy fabric that allowed one to climb, ride, and run with ease. "It was made in the Elvish District. I special-ordered it." She lifted her hem to reveal the silver pants. Instinct had told her that it might come in handy, so she'd worn her workout suit beneath her gown.

"My running shoes are in here." She patted her cape's deep pockets.

"Great. You'll need them."

As they entered the Enchanted Forest, Darling reached for the torch app on her MirrorPhone, but it wasn't necessary. The moon was so full and glorious that its beams shot through the trees, illuminating the forest floor. "Madam Maid Marian…" Darling said.

"Please, just call me Marian. *Madam Maid* is so stuffy."

"Yes, of course. Marian…" It felt strange to call a teacher by her first name, but at the same time, it felt liberating. "Why did you invite me out here?"

"You were so distracted and distant in class today. I could tell that something was weighing heavily on your mind." They stopped in a clearing and Marian set her bag on a tree stump. "When I'm feeling stressed, I like to do something active. Are you the same way?" Darling nodded. "I thought so." Marian opened her bag and pulled out a bow. "Have you ever used one of these?"

"No."

Darling remembered all those afternoons when she'd watched from the tower window while her brothers took archery lessons in the garden below. When she asked if she could try, Queen Charming said, "Bows and arrows are too dangerous for a Charming princess. You'll shoot your foot. Besides, look what happened to that nice girl, Maid Marian. She took up the sport and started robbing from the rich. She became a threat to kingdom security. I won't let that happen to you."

Darling chuckled to herself as she recalled that moment, but she didn't want to insult Marian by sharing it. She watched as Marian took out a quiver filled with arrows. They used the stump as a target. On the first dozen tries, Darling's arrows fell limply to the ground. By the thirteenth try, it sprung forward and flew. She didn't shoot her foot, but she did

manage to hit a few nearby trees before she finally made the target. "I did it!" she cried.

"You learn quickly," Marian said as she retrieved the arrow. "I'm starting to believe you can do anything if you set your mind to it."

They took a break, sitting on a bed of moss, sipping Jack Frost Glacier Water from two bottles that Marián had tucked in her bag. "I have your book," Darling told her. "I loved reading about your life with the Merry Men, but you don't talk much about your life before you met Robin Hood."

"Oh, I was a damsel, and I was told that my prince would come and I was supposed to wait for that day. And then I'd get married, become a queen, and live happily ever after."

"Same with me," Darling said. "I'm going to be in some sort of dangerous situation, but my prince will whisk me away in time. But what if he doesn't? I mean, how can I base my whole future on some anonymous dude? What if he has something else to do that day? Or what if he gets hit by a carriage and can't get to me? Am I supposed to shrug and say 'oh well, I guess this is my destiny'? I don't think so. And it's pretty frustrating that everywhere I go, I have to deal with all these boys trying to win my heart simply because I'm a Charming princess." She realized she'd been speaking very loudly. She glanced around. "I shouldn't say those sorts of things."

Marian laughed. "Don't be ashamed if you want to go off script. In my day, no one was called a Rebel. They weren't out in the open, like you kids are nowadays. But Rebels existed. Rebels have always existed. As long as there have been stories, there have been characters who refuse to stick to the outline." She replaced the cap on her water bottle, then set it aside. "If not a helpless damsel, then what do you want to be?"

"I want to be a hero." Darling had never said those words aloud. Not to anyone, not even Dexter. It was a huge confession. And it felt great. "I want to be the one to come to the rescue. To save the day."

"I think that's a noble goal," Marian said. She pulled a pair of sneakers from her bag. "But just remember, you're not really the hero if the person you're rescuing doesn't want or need to be rescued."

Darling took a long, deep breath of forest air. "You're right," she said as she thought of Dexter lying in bed, covered in blue spots. He hadn't asked for her help. And he certainly didn't need to be rescued. He had the right to write his own story. And so did she.

Marian tied her laces, then stood. "Well, how about we go for that run?"

"Yes!" Darling tossed her cape aside, then pulled her gown off over her head. She zipped up her workout jacket and slipped her feet into her running shoes.

And she ran.

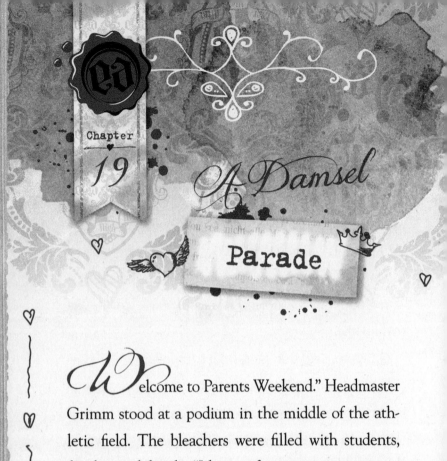

A Damsel

Parade

"Welcome to Parents Weekend." Headmaster Grimm stood at a podium in the middle of the athletic field. The bleachers were filled with students, faculty, and family. "I have a few announcements to make before we begin the opening ceremony." He tapped the microphone to make sure it was working. "Regarding parking—I'm sorry to say that the helipad is full, as is the carriage lot. There are a few spaces left behind Mr. Green Thumb's garden, but please do not park on his beloved squash. And make sure to

get your parking pass validated by one of the parking fairies." He dabbed his forehead with a handkerchief.

Darling sat in the front row of the bleachers, between Apple White and Briar Beauty. The three girls wore so much taffeta, lace, and sequins that they could have opened their own fabric store. Briar had fallen asleep on Darling's shoulder, leaving a little patch of drool. Darling nudged her awake. The Hero Training students were dragging their armor into a temporary tent that had been borrowed from Camelot. She spied Daring and Hunter, but where was Dexter? When she'd called him that morning, he'd said he was fine and that she didn't need to worry. But his voice had still sounded ragged.

Then she saw him. He was walking slowly, dressed in half his dented armor and carrying the rest. Was he still sick?

Headmaster Grimm cleared his throat, then continued. "In honor of the visiting parents, Hagatha is preparing tonight's feast." The audience groaned.

"I am told that it is a woodland stew, and I'm sure it will surprise us with its depth of flavor and interesting textures."

"Let's hope no one breaks a tooth on a twig," Apple whispered.

"After today's opening ceremony, you are welcome to visit the Cooking Class-ic classroom and try some student-made treats. The Science and Sorcery classroom will be open if you would like to see your student's lab work up close. And a mini-lecture titled "Why Sleep Is Important for a Healthy Student" will be given by Professor Rip Van Winkle in the Charmitorium," the headmaster said.

Darling turned and looked up in the bleachers. King and Queen Charming sat in the central box seats, surrounded by a contingent of Charmings— Grandpa Auspicious, Aunt Fairest, and cousins Cherished, Fearless, Breathtaking, and Beloved, to name a few. All those Charming eyes would be watching, judging, and expecting the Charming

siblings to be perfect representations of their destinies. Darling broke out in a cold sweat.

"Oh dear, you're getting shiny," Apple said. She reached into her jeweled purse and pulled out a powder puff. "Are you nervous?"

"A bit," Darling admitted.

Apple blotted Darling's nose. "Don't worry. You are the perfect princess, and everyone knows it."

Trumpets blasted and the crowd stood for the Ever After High anthem. The Pied Piper Band marched across the field, a few stray rats at their heels.

"Eew," Briar said as a rat darted out from under their bench to join the others. Once the music stopped, the audience took their seats, and Headmaster Grimm continued speaking. "We shall now have a special parade by our Damsel-In-Distressing class. Then, it's the moment you've all been waiting for, as our very own Ever After High heroes will delight you with their jousting skills!" Everyone applauded.

 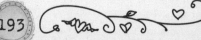

Madam Maid Marian stepped onto the field and motioned her students forward. "Here we go," Duchess said with a roll of her eyes.

For once, Madam Maid Marian had decided that they'd stick to protocol. The tradition was that the damsels would present themselves to the audience in a parade. Walking down a royal red carpet took minimal effort and required no talent whatsoever. Best of all, there was very little risk involved. The school's doctor was standing nearby in case a damsel strained her wrist from waving. "I know this seems ridiculous," Madam Maid Marian whispered to them, "so let's just get it over with."

They were dressed in their utmost finery. Layers of satin and silk. Beaded corsets and brocaded skirts. Holly looked as if she was wearing every single piece of jewelry she owned, and Briar's tiara was encrusted with too many diamonds to count. Cerise's red cape was sprinkled with gold dust, and Apple's velvet sash dragged six feet behind her. Darling kept accidentally stepping on it. "Sorry." Just then, a few

birds swooped in, picking up Apple's sash and carrying it behind her. *I wish I could get out of these heels,* Darling thought.

As the Pied Piper Band played, Sparrow Hood took the microphone, singing a screechy version of "Girl, You Are So Dutiful." The damsels walked, one at a time, down the red carpet. They smiled. They waved. They curtsied. Parents recorded the moment on their MirrorPhones. When it was Darling's turn, three boys ran onto the field, ready to propose, but they were shooed away by the headmaster.

When the parade was over, polite applause arose from the bleachers. The damsels returned to their bleacher seats. Apple and the others sighed with relief, but Darling didn't. She chewed on her lower lip and could think of only one thing—Dexter.

Headmaster Grimm took to the podium again. "Thank you, young ladies, for that display. We can all rest assured knowing that you will be the next generation of helpless damsels." Cerise growled softly under her cloak's hood. "And now the moment you've all been waiting for. Please give a rousing welcome to the heroes of Ever After High!"

A cacophony of foot stomping, whistling, and cheering arose as the heroes emerged from the tent. Each was on horseback and in full regalia. Professor Knight rode first, his swaybacked horse looking as if it might collapse at any moment. Then came Daring, his blond hair flowing in the breeze, his smile nearly blinding the onlookers. Ashlynn jumped to her feet and waved as Hunter emerged. The audience continued its wild adoration as, one by one, the Hero Training students rode past the bleachers.

Darling shifted nervously. Where was Dexter?

Professor Knight rode to the podium. Headmaster Grimm held the microphone up to the professor's white beard. "Ladies and gentlemen," the old knight said, waving his hands for silence. The crowd settled, all ears tuned to the proceedings. "I have had the privilege of instructing your squires in the traditional skills of knighthood. The chivalric code is…"

Darling stopped listening. Something wasn't right. King Charming had ordered Hunter to escort Dexter to the tournament. Hunter wouldn't fail. So why was Dexter still in the tent?

Madam Maid Marian's voice rang in her ears. *You're not really the hero if the person you're rescuing doesn't want or need to be rescued.*

Dexter didn't want her help in the tournament. But instinct told her that at that moment, he needed her.

Darling stood and flipped her hair. Professor Knight stopped midsentence. Daring froze midsmile. Even the clouds stopped moving.

While time nearly came to a standstill, Darling scrambled from the bench. She kicked off her heels, grabbing them with her right hand, and with her left hand she lifted the hem of her dress. Then she ran as fast as she could.

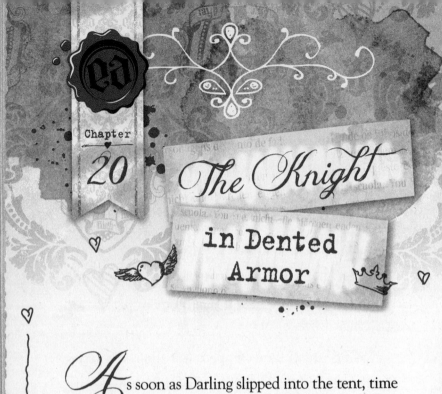

The Knight
in Dented Armor

As soon as Darling slipped into the tent, time returned to normal. Professor Knight's voice bellowed from the speakers as he rambled on and on about chivalry. He made no mention of the girl who had just streaked across the field. To those who had been suspended in time, Darling would have appeared to be nothing more than a sunbeam, or a glint from one of the jousting shields.

Dexter was sitting on a bench. He was dressed in

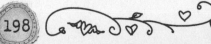

everything but his helmet. A black horse stood by his side. "What's the matter?" Darling asked, sliding onto the bench next to him. "Are you still sick?"

"No, I actually feel much better." The blue spots were gone and he didn't look one bit sleepy. His eyes, however, were not sparkling in their usual manner. They were clouded with sadness. "I'm worried. Not about throwing the match. That's the easy part. But I'm still stuck with this stupid helmet. How can Dare win if I'm riding in the wrong direction? I won't even be able to tell where I'm aiming my lance. What if I accidentally hit him?" Darling had been worried about the exact same thing all morning. "And to make matters worse, I don't even know this horse. But Hunter says it's the one I've been riding all week. I mean, the one *you've* been riding all week."

"The horse is the last thing you have to worry about." She reached over and patted Sir Gallopad's leg. "You don't have to guide him. He knows exactly what he's doing. He'll carry you safely down the field. There'll be no galloping in the wrong direction." Sir Gallopad snorted.

"Well, at least I've got that going for me," Dexter said with a half smile.

They heard cheers arise outside as Professor Knight announced the first pair of jousters.

"Are Mom and Dad out there?"

"Yes," she said. But she didn't mention the rest of the Charming clan. Dexter had a tendency to get hives when he was extra nervous, and it was nearly impossible to scratch while wearing armor, as she now knew.

"And what about…?" He gulped. "Is…is Raven out there?"

"Yep. She's in the bleachers." Darling took Dexter's hand. "Look, don't worry for one second about Raven. She told me she's not impressed by all this knight-in-shining-armor stuff. She likes boys who read."

"Really?" He smiled and—*bling!*—his eyes were sparkling once again, even behind his glasses.

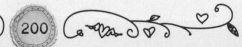

A trumpet blasted, followed by "Charge!" Darling stood. "You'd better get ready. I'll help you get on the horse."

With a sigh, Dexter took off his glasses and picked up the dented helmet. "I'm sorry you can't be the one to claim the championship," he said. "It's stupid, really, that you're not allowed. Maybe one day…" He pulled the helmet over his head. "Maybe things will change."

"You're not mad at me for pretending to be you?"

"Mad at you? Of course not." He flipped up the visor. "How could I be mad? We promised to come to each other's rescue, remember?"

It was an awkward hug, what with the plates of armor and Darling's taffeta sleeve getting caught on Dexter's gauntlet, but the hug represented words that did not need to be said. Darling and Dexter were a team. They would always have each other's backs.

While the trumpet sounded again, followed by another "Charge!" Darling grabbed the footstool

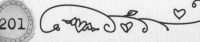

and helped guide her brother onto the horse. Just as Dexter was settled into the saddle, Daring and his steed stuck their heads into the tent.

"Hey, Dex, what's taking you so long? Are you okay?"

"Yeah, sure. Why wouldn't I be okay?"

"Look, I know this is stressful. You're not used to championships. But don't worry about getting hurt. I promise to be very careful. I'm not going to send my brother flying out of his saddle. You have my word."

"Thanks, Dare."

"Let's go. It's almost our turn." Daring and his steed turned around and disappeared from view.

"Take this," Darling said, holding up the shield. Because Dexter could barely see, it took a few moments for him to grab it. "No, that's the wrong hand." Then she picked up the lance. "Close your visor, then take this." He did.

"This thing is heavy!" He wobbled as he tried to find his balance.

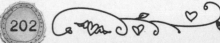

"I know you missed a few classes, but this thing is called a lance," she teased.

"Dare promised not to hurt me, but what if I hurt him? How am I going to aim this thing if I can't see?"

"Actually, I think I've figured that out," she said as she lifted the tent's flap. "Do you still trust me?"

"Yes," he said. "Whatever you've got up your sleeve, do it."

As Sir Gallopad carried Dexter to the end of the field, Darling slipped back into her shoes, then left the tent. "And now the moment we've been waiting for," Professor Knight announced. "The championship round." The cheering, whistling, and stomping reached epic proportions as Daring and his steed rode in front of the bleachers. Dexter, however, waited quietly on his end of the field. After his solo parade, Daring took his place on the opposite end.

Darling gripped the sides of her heavy skirt. How she longed to be in that saddle. To feel that moment just before the charge, adrenaline coursing through

 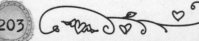

her veins, heart pounding with anticipation. Would she ever get to play the shining knight again?

The trumpet sounded. "Charge!" Daring yelled. Dexter forgot to holler and almost toppled backward as Sir Gallopad took off. The horses galloped down the field. Daring looked the expert, sure and graceful, his polished armor gleaming in the afternoon sun. Dexter did his best to hold steady in the saddle. The sun was not so kind to him, as it highlighted the dents in his armor. But it didn't matter what he looked like, for at that moment, Dexter was showing great courage. To face such a task, without being able to see two feet in front of him, was truly brave. She smiled with pride.

Then she started chewing on her lip again. Because the next few seconds would prove critical.

Sir Gallopad and Daring's steed made their way along the fence, closing the distance between the two riders. The crowd fell silent. Horse hooves beat the earth. Darling's heart pounded in her ears. She didn't dare look at the bleachers to watch her parents' reactions. If she took her eyes off her brothers, she might miss the exact moment when she'd need to enact her plan.

Closer and closer the riders came. Daring aimed his lance. Dexter didn't. Closer, closer…this was it. Darling flipped her hair.

While the world hung in suspension, Darling grabbed the step stool and set it next to Sir Gallopad. It was odd to see her beloved horse frozen midstride. She gave him a quick pat, then climbed up to inspect the situation. From the looks of it, Daring's lance was perfectly positioned to hit Dexter's shield. But Dexter's lance was way off target. It would certainly hit the other horse's left flank. Standing on tiptoe, Darling adjusted Dexter's arms and his grip, repositioning his lance so that it was aiming at the edge of Daring's shield. It would be a hit, but not a winning one. And hopefully, no one would get hurt. "Good luck," she said. Then, stool in hand, she ran back to the edge of the field and waited. Time moved forward.

Whack!

As Dexter's lance grazed Daring's shield, Daring's lance hit Dexter's shield pinpoint center. The tip broke off and flew toward the bleachers. A girl screamed with delight as she caught it. The crowd cheered. King Charming and the entire Charming clan leaped to their feet. Daring was the champion, once again, and Dexter was second best. For the first time in her life, Darling truly felt as if she might faint. She sank onto the stool.

A bouquet of flowers landed at her feet.

The world was in order.

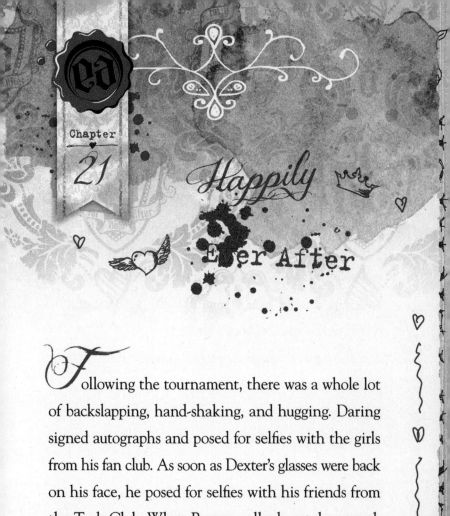

Chapter 21

Happily Ever After

Following the tournament, there was a whole lot of backslapping, hand-shaking, and hugging. Daring signed autographs and posed for selfies with the girls from his fan club. As soon as Dexter's glasses were back on his face, he posed for selfies with his friends from the Tech Club. When Raven walked past, he waved. She waved back. The horses returned to the stables to be watered and fed. Darling kissed Sir Gallopad's muzzle and promised him that they'd ride very soon.

"Just as it should be," King Charming said as he

held Daring's trophy above his head. "I never had a doubt about the outcome. Championship comes naturally to Daring. It always has."

"Don't forget about Dexter," Queen Charming said. "He came in second place."

The king lowered the trophy and turned to Dexter. "Yes, indeed. I used to worry about all that time you spent reading and gaming on the Mirror Network, son, but you did a fine job today. I'm very proud."

"Thanks, Dad." Dexter smiled.

Darling watched the goings-on from the sidelines. Since the tournament's conclusion, she'd had to fend off three marriage proposals. Luckily, the Charming cousins had come to her rescue, and had carried the starstruck boys off the field. The crowd was clearing. The other princesses were walking back to campus to get ready for the evening feast. But Darling wanted to talk to Dexter, to make sure he was okay.

"Hey there." Betty Bunyan strode up to Darling. She was dressed in jeans and a leather motorcycle

jacket with painted flames that matched her flame tattoos. Her black braids were tied back in a red bandanna, and the diamond in her nostril glimmered. "I got back last night and made this." She handed Darling a new helmet. "It should fit right over Dexter's glasses. Where is he?" Darling pointed to the podium, where Professor Knight was handing small ribbons to the squires, including Dexter. "Oh, I guess I'm too late. Sorry about that."

"It's okay. It all worked out," Darling told her with a devilish smile. "In fact, it was one of the best weeks of my life. I mean, of Dexter's life. He was the one wearing his helmet. And doing all the jousting. Of course." Betty raised her eyebrows. It looked as if she was about to ask a question, so Darling hurriedly changed the subject. "How's your dad, by the way?"

"He's back home, but that bunion was the size of a toad. It's going to be a while before he's back on his feet." She took a coupon from her pocket. "Say, I feel bad that I couldn't get to Dexter's armor in time for the tournament. Would you let him know that he can bring it in for a complimentary buff and shine? And I'll give him half off on dent and ding removal."

"Sure," Darling said, taking the coupon. "Thanks."

As Betty walked away, Queen Charming approached. "Hello, Darling," she said, placing a gentle kiss on her daughter's cheek. "Why are you carrying that helmet?"

"It's for Dexter," she explained.

"I see." The queen picked a stray leaf from Darling's hair. "I know your brothers always get all the attention, but I wanted you to know how very proud we were when you walked in the damsel parade today. You are the epitome of the perfect Charming princess." She held out a small package, wrapped in pink paper with a pink bow. "A gift to commemorate this lovely day."

"Really?" Darling set the helmet at her feet, then peeled back the wrapping paper to reveal a copy of *Secrets of the Sherwood Forest.* Darling tried to hide her surprise. Was this some sort of test?

"I thought your old copy might be getting worn out by now," Queen Charming said. "Oh, don't look so

alarmed, Darling. It's one of my favorite books, too. And look, I had it signed." She opened to the title page.

To Darling Charming,
May your time in the forest always
be glorious.
Forever after,
        Madam Maid Marian

"Marian and I were roommates during our years at Ever After High," Queen Charming explained. Her expression took on a faraway, dreamy look. "Those were thrilling days."

Thrilling? That wasn't a word that a traditional damsel usually uttered. Darling hugged the book to her chest. "Thank you. This is the best present ever."

The queen cupped Darling's face in her hands. "And you are my best present ever." Then she stepped away, patting her beehive hair to make sure it was firmly in place. "It is time to freshen up for the feast. I'll go get your father."

Dexter stumbled over. He was still wearing his armor and had accessorized it with a big, goofy grin. "I don't know how we did it, but I got second place. Did you see my ribbon? And did you see Raven? She waved at me." He gestured to the new helmet. "Is that what I think it is?"

"Yep. Betty made it."

He handed Darling his old helmet, then pulled the new one over his head, glasses and all. "Fits perfectly! I can see!"

The old helmet was warm in Darling's hand. She looked at it longingly. "Hey, Dex? Can I have this?"

"I guess so," he said with a shrug. "But I don't know what you'll do with it."

"Oh, I have some ideas." One day, the time would be right to let the world see her true self, and on that day, a helmet might come in handy. "And I was thinking, could I borrow your armor every once in a while, just so I can stroll through the village without having to deal with any potential suitors?"

"Yeah, okay." He pulled off the new helmet and tucked it under his arm. "What's that?"

"It's a new copy of my favorite book. You left the library copy for me outside my bedroom when we were little. Remember?"

"No, I didn't."

"You didn't? Then who did?"

Dexter and Darling turned and watched their parents walk arm in arm across the field. The queen looked every bit the perfect royal lady. She moved with grace, her head held high, not a hair out of place. Darling could still feel her mother's hands cupping her face. It had been a warm embrace, but there had also been something odd about her mother's hands. They'd felt a bit rough. As if…

…as if they were covered in calluses.

Darling tossed her head back and laughed.

Acknowledgments

For this, my third Ever After High book, I have many people to thank, most especially my editorial team at Little, Brown. Erin Stein, I miss you, but you left me in the highly capable hands of Rachel Poloski, Mary-Kate Gaudet, and Pam Garfinkel. Together, we four shall continue to explore this fairytale world and all the crazy, fun stuff that comes with it. Huge thanks also to my lovely copy editor, Christine Ma, and the rest of the LB staff—Andrew Smith, Kristina Aven, Victoria Stapleton, Barbara Bakowski, Mara Lander, and Véronique Sweet—for your continued support!

To the creative team at Mattel: Thanks so much to Venetia Davie, Julia Phelps, Ryan Ferguson, Charnita Belcher, Nicole Corse, Darren Sander, Emily Kelly, MJ Offen, Sally Eagle, Lara Dalian, Talia Rodgers, Audu Paden, and Robert Rudman for helping me find my way in their amazing world.

Michael, you deserve a throne.

Bob, Walker, and Isabelle, as always, you are my Happily Ever Afters.

About the Author

$\mathscr{S}$uzanne Selfors feels like a Royal on some days and a Rebel on others. She's written many books for kids, including the Smells Like Dog series and the Imaginary Veterinary series.

She has two charming children and lives in a magical island kingdom, where she hopes it is her destiny to write stories forever after.

*W*hat would you do if you were
Darling Charming or Dexter Charming?

Rewrite the story with a
Destiny Do-Over Diary!